WHISPERS IN
THE GRAVEYARD

Also by Theresa Breslin

Kezzie
A Homecoming for Kezzie

WHISPERS IN THE GRAVEYARD

THERESA BRESLIN

Best wishes
to
Kay

Theresa Breslin

MAMMOTH

This book is for John, and Alison, and Margaret, and many, many more.

First published in Great Britain
by Methuen Children's Books Ltd
Published 1995 by Mammoth
an imprint of Reed International Books Ltd
Michelin House, 81 Fulham Road, London SW3 6RB
and Auckland, Melbourne, Singapore and Toronto

Reprinted 1995 (three times)

ISBN 0 7497 2388 2

A CIP catalogue record for this title
is available from the British Library

Printed and bound in Great Britain
by Cox & Wyman Ltd, Reading, Berkshire

Chapter 1

My footprints track across the faint dew still lying on the grass. My boots crunch heavily on the hard gravel path, and I'm talking to myself as I walk, school bag bumping on my back. But the residents lodged on either side of these avenues won't complain about the noise.

They're dead.

Every one of them.

Their headstones march beside me. I stop to look at one of my favourites. A weaver. There is a carving of a leopard with a shuttle in its mouth. The animal's head is black with age, its stone roar a silent echo in a grey Scottish kirkyard. The leopard used to be on the crest of the Guild of Weavers. My dad told me.

Early morning mist comes creeping between the gravestones. I shiver. It's because I'm cold though, not scared.

Not yet.

I touch the old tinker's grave. A ram's horns and crossed spoons. That's how I know a tinker is buried there. The carvings and designs on the stones tell you. They all mean something. My dad told me to listen and I would hear the crackle of the gypsies' campfire, the black pot swinging just above the flames.

I wish words on paper were as easy to read and understand.

There's a big stone vase monument on this path, with a draped cloth and a trailing vine. That's a symbol from the Bible. Dad read out a psalm to me one night. 'Fruitful vine, and olive plants.' I liked the sound of those words, rolling around inside my head.

Masons used trees and plants a lot on memorials, ivy and

bay leaf, lilies, thistles and roses. It's traditional. They used to strew flowers on graves in ancient times, and grow evergreens in kirkyards.

I leave the path and cross the grass past the pile of stones that make up the cairn memorial and go towards the back wall. It's empty and bare here. Only a single rowan tree growing, and just behind it the dyke is half broken down. I can go through the wood at the other side of the graveyard past the river, on my way to school.

I climb up and pull away some of the stones. There's a ledge where I can lie, out of sight. I've got stuff stashed here. Emergency rations for when I dog off school and can't go home. An old blanket, comic books, biscuits, cans of juice. I unwrap the plastic covering and take out a soft digestive. This will have to be breakfast. It was Old Mother Hubbard time in our house this morning. Not one of our better weekends, you might say. Dad hasn't had any work for a while, not even casual.

You get used to having nothing, though. Weeks and weeks on the giro. Toasted cheese, spaghetti on toast, toast and beans, french toast, scrambled eggs on toast, toast and jam, toast and butter, toast and marg. Dry toast. Toast.

One night we were watching a film on the telly. Just the two of us. About the British Army. An old black and white one. *Tunes of Glory* or something. And there was this bit where they were in the officers' mess, and this guy leapt to his feet and went, 'Gentlemen, the King. I give you the toast.' And I just looked over at Dad, and at the same minute he was looking at me, and both of us laughed, really loud, and the next thing we're hysterical, rolling about on the floor. And then he sits up, wipes tears from his eyes and punches me on the shoulder. We sit on the couch and watch the rest of the film together, me kind of small and skinny leaning up against his muscley arm.

That's the way it is with us sometimes. For ages after, if things were grim, one of us would just go, 'Gentlemen, I give you the toast.' And the next thing we'd be laughing ourselves silly.

Then he gets a bit of work on the black and there's money coming in. And it's good times all round. *Happy days are here again, the world is full of cheer again.* And he's the all singing, all dancing, ever popular parent.

Let's go to the supermarket.

Let's treat ourselves at the chippy.

Let's just have a bottle of something from the off-licence.

'No.'

'Just a couple of cans.'

'No.'

'Sol, old son, you're being a bit of a bore. D'ye know that?'

'No.'

'I can handle it.'

Oh no you can't. Oh yes I can. Oh no you can't. Oh yes I can. What do you think children? All of you who believe in fairy stories, clap your hands.

It was always like that with the shopping. When I was smaller he would go and have 'a quick one' while she and I trailed around the supermarket. Then we'd have to hang about the car park waiting for him. One time he was away so long all the frozen food packages had melted. Our plastic carrier bags were full of soggy cardboard boxes, water running out the bottom. She started yelling as soon as she saw him coming towards us, all smiles and waving happily. He just turned round and walked away. I'm sure that's when she finally decided to leave.

She did give me a choice. 'Come or stay,' she said.

Some choice.

I stare at the sky. It's a darkening blue colour. A bit like my weekend. I've started to count my days in colours, from bright, clean white, all the way through to fiery, angry red. Maybe I should have gone with her. I wouldn't be having so many days with bad colours now.

I put my stuff away and cover it up. It'll be quite safe.

Hardly anyone visits here. It's too old, y'see. No one buried here would have any relatives left alive.

At least that's what I thought.

Once, though, a woman came. One of those arty types. You know. With coloured scarves and long skirts and ear-rings. She did rubbings from the tombstones and then wandered off peering at things. I liked her pictures. Didn't mind her being there either. Didn't try to scare her off. The way she touched the stones with her palms and fingers, I could tell she was listening to them. She came so close to my place I could hear her talking to herself.

'Strange, nobody buried at this end. Can't see why not. Must be a reason . . . Nothing growing either.' She frowned and put her head on one side. 'One single rowan tree.' She reached out her hand to touch the smooth silver bark, and then stopped. She shivered and moved away.

That's when I first realised nothing grew at my end. I suppose I should have wondered why that part of the wall had fallen away and had never been repaired, especially as all the rest was in fairly good order. Not even lichen and moss in the cracks to bind the stones together. But I didn't. Just as well. I might have been tempted to start poking about, and it could have been me that got it first.

The way it turned out someone else was there before me. Though I did get involved eventually. Not particularly wanting to. But then if I hadn't, things would have been very much worse.

A lot more people might have died.

Chapter 2

Enter Warrior Watkins, scourge of the squaddies, specially selected to take the top juniors and lick them into shape for going up to high school. He's collecting in our weekend work.

He lingers at Sharon Fraser's desk. She sits in the front row, right under his eye. All teeth and lipstick and legs.

'I hope I've done enough.' She gives him the thousand-candle-power mega-smile.

It's a ten-page exercise in perfect copy. He grunts as he looks at it. Disappointed, he takes the folder from her and moves on to find a victim. It's cool. I'm OK. I've copied my homework in the cloakroom from my pal Peter.

'Make some mistakes for God's sake,' said Peter, eating an apple and leaning over my shoulder. 'He's not totally thick.'

Peter's tall and broad and good-looking and smart. I don't know why he decided to be friends with me. One day in Primary Five he stopped in the middle of bashing me to bits and said, 'You know, you're hardly worth the effort. Pathetic.' He watched as I silently cleaned my bleeding nose and fixed my clothes. Then he said, 'Right enough, maybe it's me that's pathetic.' He picked up my school bag and carried it home. And that was it. From then on he was an ally. Best buddy. My mate. Peter.

And do I need him now? Do I ever. It's do-your-diary time. My left hand crooked around my book, the page at right angles to the desk, I scrawl out my best effort.

'Bloody baboon,' hisses Watkins as he goes past.

My face burns and my fingers tighten on the pencil. The words start to blur. I stop and look at the squiggles I've made. Has it come out right this time? Peter'll check this sentence.

Good old Peter. Thou art Peter and upon this rock I will build my . . .

I shove it across and Peter gives it a quick look-see. He rolls his eyes, shakes his head and marks an X in sign language on the desk.

It's a bad one.

I stare at the page in a desperate panic. What's wrong with it? Sometimes I get bs and ds mixed up, or words back to front.

Watkins is prowling back, metre stick swishing, searching for an outlet for that little fire he's banked up. Sharon Fraser has a lot to answer for.

He brings it down with a crash beside me.

'Let's have a look, Solly boy, shall we? What is it this morning? Egyptian hieroglyphics? Martian?'

'Ignore him,' mutters Peter.

And I try. Really I do.

My jotter is dangling from Watkins' fingers. He sneers as he reads it out. 'No saturbay I was a footdall maSh . . .' His face is pushed up against mine, cheese and oniony breath smells in my face. Crepey skin sags around his eyes, little red broken veins make crazed lines on the whites.

Don't stand so stand so stand so close to me

'You are a lazy stupid boy.' Thump, thump, on the desk. Fingers whorled and nicotined clench the ruler. 'Nobody in my class turns in work like this.' Thump, thump. 'Nobody.'

I wonder what would happen if I actually told Watkins about my weekend? This time Dad's bender lasted all Saturday and Sunday. I eventually got him to bed at four o'clock this morning. I looked in on him before I left for school. He had peed on the sheets. There was nothing I could do. I didn't have the time and he's too big for me to move anyway.

Where he'd got the stuff from I don't know. No matter

how broke we are he always manages to get his hands on some more booze. Charm, that's what he's got. By the bucket. Neighbours lend him money. Shops give him tick. Pubs, where he's been barred only weeks before, will end up serving him. 'Just the one, mind.'

Once he was missing for hours and I found him at our town's big hotel in amongst a wedding party. Everybody thought he was someone else's uncle, He'd been getting free drink all afternoon and evening. When I arrived he was cracking jokes and telling them wild stories about his life in the Far East. The Far East! The farthest East he's ever been is Edinburgh.

He's good with the stories though. Maybe that's why I stayed with him. Telling them, reading them, making them up. The sounds of the words spilling out of his mouth and into my heart. Playing all the parts. Gollum and Gandalf the Grey. Capering around my bedroom at two in the morning, pulling the quilt from the bed to make a hobbit hole on the floor.

I suppose I fell in love with him then, and hated her, my mother, shrieking from the door. 'You've woken that child again. You drunken fool!'

Well, who's a fool now? Tom fool. April fool. Play the fool.

'OUT!' Watkins is yelling.

He takes my exercise book and chucks it across the classroom. Suits me. I shrug and shoulder the ruckie. Peter grimaces. The rest stay low. With me gone he'll be looking for another target. One of the girls probably.

Melanie Wilson. She gives me a tiny sympathetic wave as I pass her. Poor Mousey Melly. She'll be in tears before morning break.

Now I'm in the school yard. Its emptiness accuses me. I'm supposed to stand out until first bell, but I'm not stopping here this morning. I look back as I slouch away through the gate and down the road. Take your time. Don't hurry. Make with the real slow insolence, just in case Watkins is watching. The school windows stare back at me. Stupid, blank and vacant.

Like my dad's eyes when he's totally crashed.

God, I hate that place.

Chapter 3

I count the money in my anorak pocket. Enough for a burger.

I'll need to get off the street quick. Can't hang about. The local Miami Vice know me as a school dogger. They'll round me up and take me back, which would probably involve three officers and two cars. Meanwhile the Post Office might be getting turned over.

Yes, your lordship, I was being questioned as to the rightful ownership of the aforesaid crunchie bar, submitted by the procurator as evidence, Exhibit A, when the getaway car accelerated away from the Post Office and screeched past us doing ninety in a built-up area.

Did the constable say anything at the time?

Yes, your lordship, he said. Some of those old age pensioners are in a real hurry to get their allowance, aren't they?

I climb over the graveyard wall and drop down on the other side.

Something is wrong.

The soil beneath the wall has been disturbed.

Someone has been here.

They have left equipment close by. Tarpaulins and scaffolding. Heavy boot prints stamped in the earth, gouge marks on the grass. I don't like this. Further down the path there are notices pinned up. I pull one down and stuff it in my pocket to look at later.

What's going on?

I wander about, restless and agitated. There is a great disquiet all around me. Why?

I lean against the tombstones. The familiar carvings of winged souls and hourglasses are old friends. These markings

I can read and understand. I run my fingers over them. The crumbling old stone, mellow and marmalade-coloured, is warm beneath my fingers. The contours are soft and welcome my touch. The later grey slabs stand firm, their faces dark and strong. I reach up to the old carved urn. The cloth draped over it is smooth and reassuring, soft folds falling, falling . . .

There is a flowering cherry right beside it. I gaze high through its branches. Its full frothy head is a spring song in the sky.

I go back to the wall and get myself comfortable on my ledge, with my burger and comic. The sun is on my face. I close my eyes.

Then I hear the sound of a heavy engine. I peer out through the stones. There's a District Council van driving through the bottom gate. Workies start piling out with picks and shovels. A larger car following them bumps up on the grass verge. Two official-looking plonkers get out and stride up the path towards me.

I cower down lower in my hiding place. They can't possibly see me, can they? They stop a few metres short of my wall.

'Drainage,' says the smaller man. He's wrapped up in a tan raincoat, hands stuck in his pockets. He rocks back and forth on his heels and then stamps his feet a couple of times. 'Drainage, Professor Miller. That's going to be a big problem.'

'Mmmm?' The one called Professor Miller seems more interested in the gravestones. He has stopped to examine one. He traces the line of the pattern with his fingers, his hands gliding lightly along the surface like a doctor's, searching, probing. 'This is extremely interesting.' He has the trace of an Irish accent in his voice. 'What is the history of this place?'

'It was a burial ground attached to a small church. There are only a few stones of the ancient kirk left in one corner. It

14

became overcrowded and was closed some time ago. I believe its origins are pre-medieval.'

'Yes, that's apparent.' The professor takes a small eyeglass from his pocket. He indicates the west wall. 'Some of those pieces of masonry are Pictish symbol stones which have been broken up and used as coping. It's unbelievable how some local authorities allow a national heritage to be destroyed.'

'Exactly so,' said the other man pompously. 'We won't be allowing that to happen here. That's why we've called you in for expert opinion. The council is building a new bridge across the river and we have to change the road alignment and divert the course of the water. All of the graves will have to be relocated. At first we thought we'd just collect all the headstones together and pile them up somewhere.' He waved his arm around vaguely.

'Did you?' asked the professor quietly.

'But of course this council likes to do things properly,' the official went on hurriedly. 'We recognise the historic value of these . . . er . . . things. So if you can undertake the special study required as soon as possible, and advise us of the best ways to preserve our cultural heritage, we'll get on with moving the bodies.'

The two men are moving along the path as they speak. The professor stops at the cairn and, picking up one or two of the stones, he examines them carefully with his magnifier.

'How long do you think it will take you?' asks the official.

'A few weeks anyway,' says the professor slowly. He keeps one of the stones in his hand as he walks all the way round the monument.

'Good. Good. That's what we envisaged. We'll start clearing the vegetation immediately and then we can start work on the exhumations.'

'Mr Frame,' says Professor Miller, 'have you had a good look at this particular memorial?'

'Not especially, no.'

'Then I suggest you do. I'm afraid you may have a serious

15

problem to contend with.' Professor Miller replaces the stone in its original position. 'Have you heard the expression "Cholera Ground" used in connection with old burial places?' he asks.

'Cholera Ground?' Mr Frame laughs. 'Cholera is a foreign disease. You don't get cholera in Scotland.'

'Not any more perhaps,' says the professor, 'because now we have a clean water supply. But in the early part of the nineteenth century it killed thousands of people. However the "Cholera Ground" in churchyards wasn't used exclusively for victims of that disease. It was known as such because that was the most common disease from which people died. In actual fact it was a general name given to a special area set aside in kirkyards for the victims of any epidemic. Due to the lack of medical facilities, when pestilence struck, whole communities could be wiped out in a matter of days. Most corpses were laid to rest uncoffined. There wasn't the money or indeed the time to do anything else. And these areas were known as the "Cholera Ground".'

The professor breathes on his eyeglass, then polishes it carefully.

'Many parishes held annual inspections of the turf over the ground used to ensure it remained undisturbed,' he went on. 'They feared the virus would escape. Sometimes they used a cairn of stones as a memorial, hoping to seal the ground and prevent further outbreaks.'

'That's very interesting, but as you said, cholera was caught by drinking bad water. It's not infectious,' said Mr Frame.

'Cholera isn't, that's true,' replied the professor. 'But there was another far more deadly epidemic in Scotland. This pestilence visited the country until the late 1880s. A highly contagious virus in which the infection is carried on the skin in tiny pustules or blisters which form into scabs. The virus can survive in these dried-up scabs for many years.'

He puts his eyeglass back in his jacket pocket and then

16

points to the large cairn of stones directly in front of them.

'I suggest that you check the burial records for this kirkyard. When you do, I think you'll find that lying under that mound is a mass grave for the victims of smallpox.'

Chapter 4

'What?' Mr Frame steps back sharply. 'You're not serious.'

'I'm very serious,' says Professor Miller, 'and in the light of what else I've noticed here, I would advise you to take extreme caution before you begin uncovering any graves.'

'Why? What's wrong?' The council official's head jerks as he looks quickly around him.

'There are rules and regulations covering interments, and I think that they have not been adhered to in this burial ground. For example, graves or lairs had to be at least one and a half feet from a wall. Look,' the professor indicates a row of headstones, 'those are clearly not.' He kicks his foot gently against the long side of a mounded oblong of grass.

'Coffins are also supposed to be three or four feet down from the surface. I don't think these are.'

'Why aren't they?' Mr Frame's voice is worried. 'Surely there were inspectors to ensure things were done properly?'

The professor shrugs. 'Not always. This appears to have been a smaller church group, away from the main town. They probably did everything themselves, from laying out bodies to digging the actual grave.'

He walks further along the wall to where the earth was bare. 'What is also worrying me is this part here. You say the cemetery was closed due to overcrowding?'

Mr Frame nods.

'Well,' says Professor Miller, 'if they weren't observing the Home Office rules for spacing out coffins, it may be that, in the attempt to bury relatives beside each other, they were doing something which I've come across in other small country kirkyards.'

'Which is?'

'Breaking up older buried coffins and tipping the contents into the opened trench to make more room. See this bluish-black colour of the earth all around here? That denotes the presence of decaying corpses.'

Mr Frame takes a handkerchief from his pocket and covers his mouth. 'I suppose if we consult the Record of Burials, it would tell us what they've actually done.'

The professor laughs. 'I doubt if they've kept an accurate note. Our ancestors weren't as bureaucracy-ridden as we've become.'

'You said "our ancestors",' Mr Frame enquires. 'Do you have relatives here?'

'Yes, from a long long time ago,' says the professor. 'It's one of the reasons I accepted this commission. My wife and daughter always wanted to visit Scotland.'

They are approaching my end of the kirkyard. I breathe quiet and shallow among the stones.

'*Sorbus aucuparia*.' The professor reaches out to touch a leaf of my tree and then withdraws his hand.

'Mountain Ash,' says Mr Frame.

Professor Miller puts his head on one side. 'Do you notice it is the only living thing at this end?'

'Plenty of dead, though,' jokes Mr Frame.

'Actually no . . .' The professor is thoughtful. 'Not even the dead rest here.'

He frowns and turns slowly to face the sun. 'At first I thought it was to do with the custom of burying people on an east-west line. Scotland used to be a very God-fearing country, so in many cases the headstone was placed at the west end of the plot.' He gives a small smile. 'It was believed that the Lord's second coming would be as the sun rises, from the east, so you would wish to be laid facing Him in preparation for your resurrection. The church itself was usually built at the northern end, not in the centre, so that no one could be shamed by being buried in the shadows of the

19

northern side. If there was such an area it would be kept for suicides, bastards, criminals and vagrants. These people wouldn't have tombstones and that's why, usually, the north side of an old graveyard will have no memorials.'

'So that is why there is nothing here?'

'Except . . .' said Professor Miller. 'The church remains are in the right-hand corner. Which means that this isn't the north side . . . and . . . this part is not just bare, it's devoid of anything . . . of everything. Of life . . . and . . . death.'

Mr Frame laughs nervously.

And again, suddenly, the realisation is in my mind. Nothing flourishes here. The rowan is the only single thing that exists. Living or dead. And even the tree is strangely still. Now it is springtime and no bird has made its nest among its branches. In the autumn no bird came to eat the red rowan berries. I remember quite clearly last year, when they cascaded onto the ground, small and round and ripe, no ant or insect ate them. They lay until, rotting, they returned to the soil.

The two men move away down towards the gate. I hear Mr Frame say, 'I think I'll notify our environmental health department and get them down here immediately. They can decide what to do.' He paused for a minute.

'We'll have to wait for their clearance. Although there may be some work the squad can get on with meantime. Removing that tree for example.'

He calls to the foreman and they have a brief discussion. The workies take their tools and clamber back inside the van.

They are gone.

Silence.

But for how long?

I stand high on the wall. I touch my face; salt tears are there. They are going to destroy my place. I will have no refuge now. Even the criminals and beggars got a place of rest. Not me. I lean far out over the wall and grab a branch of the tree to swing myself down.

An edge cuts into me and tears the surface of my skin as I land at the base of the tree. The rope-thick roots rush up against my body and I roll over onto the soft earth. I see a gash in the sleeve of my jacket. Liquid red squeezes through. A few drops of my blood spill and are quickly swallowed up into the dark soil. I stand up shakily and suddenly, impulsively, I wrap my arms around its solid trunk.

The recoil sends me staggering backwards, dazed and stupefied. As though it had leapt to life beneath my grasp, had become a writhing throbbing snake, slithering against my body.

I dab at my arm. Blood makes me faint and dizzy. That's it. That explains my feeling of strange revulsion.

I stagger to my feet. I must get away. I take, though I do not know this, what will be my last look at its pearl-white skin and grey-green leaves. My doomed mountain ash.

Later, but it was really too late then. Far, far too late, I found out that rowan trees were planted to ward off evil.

Chapter 5

'You've hidden it. Where is it?'

He's rummaging through the bottom kitchen cupboards as I come in the back door. Fancy dishes, cake plates, water jugs and a decorated fruit bowl are strewn around him on the floor. Emblems of our former family life.

'Dunno what you mean.' I drop my rucksack on the floor and edge past him, picking my way among the debris. Cloth napkins, a flower vase. Things we've not used in months. Not since she left.

I slink into the hall and through to the living room. Close the door softly. Switch the telly on and squat down.

Game show. Soap. Cartoons. Talk show. News.

I flick back to the cartoons. I can watch them with the sound down.

Bright colours like my comics. Fills my head. There's light and dark and noise, movement and colour, quick and fast. It blots everything else out. Except . . .

It's better when you do it for yourself. Like . . . inside your head. You know. Make the story happen yourself. The way you want it to be. They spoil it on the telly sometimes, people don't look right, make stupid remarks that don't fit in. But words, words are different. I heard someone reading poetry on the radio once. The phrases stayed inside me for weeks, exploding in my head, thrusting and twisting in my gut.

The noise from the kitchen is getting louder. Things are being thrown. I put my head in my hands. He is getting worse. Definitely. The weekend firecracker has usually fizzled out by Monday afternoon.

There is an almighty bang from against the wall. I stretch over and turn the volume on the TV up a bit. I'm hoping the noise will cover me to get safely upstairs. I turn the door handle silently. Walking on the sides of my feet softly down the hall. Almost at the stairs now.

The kitchen door crashes open.

'You know where it is, don't you?' he demands thickly. His body fills the doorway.

I breathe slowly. Once. Twice. My sludge-coloured day is streaked with blood-orange.

'There's none left. You finished it all.'

I'm watching him carefully. My eyes on his hands. The trick is in the timing.

Get ready.

Knowing when to move is as important as knowing which way to go.

'You'd better tell me.' He points his finger in my face. His bulk has blotted out any light in the passageway.

I shake my head slowly and move backwards. He comes at me then, arms swinging. I duck.

Red alert.

Sometimes being wee and skinny is a bonus. I'm round behind him and into the kitchen before he knows it. I grab my rucksack and scramble out the back door. A crashing noise behind me. Shattered glass showers the path.

I make the lane and I don't look back.

Have to stay out for a few hours at least. I'll go to Peter's house for a bit. His mum will be at work.

His two younger sisters are squabbling in the living room. We go into his kitchen to make sandwiches.

'Where'd you end up today?' he asks me. 'I searched about for you at lunch time.'

'Here and there.' I'm offhand. No one knows my secret place. 'How was your day with W.W?'

'The usual. He had Melly blubbing away ten minutes after you left.' Peter pulls some slices of bread from the plastic-wrapped loaf on the work top. He stops, with his hand half out of the bag. 'You know, copying my work, Sol . . . I don't mind, but . . . you'll never learn anything that way.

I take out two mugs, spoon in sugar and add milk. 'Don't care,' I say quickly. 'Was Watkins bothered that I didn't come back?'

'Na.' Peter is smearing jam and peanut butter on the bread. He waves the knife at me. 'I've told you before. He's not supposed to send you out of class like that. He would get into trouble if he was found out. You should get your dad to report him.'

His eyes meet mine. He must know. We only live a few streets apart. He hands me my piece, not looking at me now.

His mum comes in lugging a supermarket bag full of shopping.

'What a mess!' she says, picking up our mugs and the jar of peanut butter from the kitchen table. 'Come on, Pete, lend a hand.' She gives him the potato peeler and a bag of potatoes.

He mumps and moans a bit, but you can see that they're used to working together. She clears the rest of the table and begins to set out plates and dishes. She takes the wrapping off a packet of cold meat and starts to put a couple of slices on each plate. Suddenly she stops and looks at me.

'Oh,' she says, hesitating. She reaches for another plate from the cupboard. 'Want to stay for dinner?' she asks.

'No,' I say quickly. 'I can't. My dad's got something ready.'

She shrugs. 'Sure?' she says. The plate is already back in its place.

I nod.

Bright smile, her. Bright smile, me.

Her eyes meet Peter's. They both look away.

I leave Peter's house and take the main road. There are still some crisps and biscuits in my bundle of stuff at the graveyard. I nip in through the main gate and along the edge of the wall.

Evening is closing in. That kind of grey-blue slow gloaming that you get in Scotland at this time of year. Late spring melting into summer. In the kirkyard everything is settling down for the night. The midges in a dancing swarm beneath the old monkey-puzzle. The birds singing, warbling and fussing about. The leaves of the older evergreens are dark and leathery. Thistle and briar choke the little thickets clustered at the foot of the trees.

The workmen have been back. Some of the horizontal slabs have been moved and stacked at one end. They are marked and labelled. I walk over to look at them.

My footsteps scrape the gravel.

I stop.

I hear something.

A soft movement behind me.

Chapter 6

A skitter of stones in the half dark. Shadows move towards me.

God! What?

Stupid. Stupid. Nothing.

I hear the stumbling conversations of a group of teenagers. I glide quietly off the path.

'Open a can, for f's sake.'

I slide, cunning and sure of my own territory, behind an upright slab. Whatever they're drinking or sniffing makes them cocksure. Confident but uneasy at the same time.

'Can't come here again. They've padlocked the gate.'

They stop to light up. Right beside me. Gathered at my altar.

'Nothing a pair of pliers can't solve.' The lit end of a cigarette arcs in the darkness.

'Dunno. Probably be a night-watch.'

'I don't like this place any more.' A girl's voice. 'Something creepy about it.'

The hand leaning on the top of my tombstone moves down as its owner changes position.

I remain rock-like. A stone image frozen for ever. But, very slowly, I reach out my tongue . . . A cold lizard. A snake. Coiling round the outstretched fingers.

The shriek is absolutely satisfying. The best thing I've felt for ages.

'What? What is it?' someone yells. But nobody is answering as they all scatter and are away.

Now the place is mine again. But nothing is as it was. There is mess and desecration everywhere. Turf has been marked out and cut, sods lifted. There are ropes looped round some of the upright statues. Other gravestones have been loosened at the edges. The branches of the cherry tree have been lopped.

Unease and disquiet vibrates in my head.

The earth near my part of the wall is churned up.

I see why.

The air I breathe into my lungs seems thick and cold. There is a length of chain around the rowan tree, cutting into its flesh. They have tried to pull it out with the van, or perhaps a tractor, but it has held fast.

Not all of it though.

It is half out of the earth. But the roots reach back. Roots that haven't seen the light of day for many, many years. Thick as a man's arm, they twist back down into the bowels of the earth, pale as a slug under a stone. The soil is a strange colour. Whiteish, like drifting sand, or ash. It's dry and dusty and blowing about a bit now in the wind. I turn my head. I hadn't felt any breeze. There is none. I look again. It's as though the ground is moving, shifting and restless like the sea.

But then that happens to me when I stare at something and try to concentrate. Pages of writing shudder before my eyes. The print struggles in front of me, swimming awkwardly on the lines.

There's nothing wrong with my eyesight though. I've had my eyes tested.

Dozens of times.

I don't have bad eyesight.

Had my hearing tested too.

I don't have poor hearing.

Or MS.

Or ME.

I've been tested for things which most people have never even heard of. They all come up clear.

They told my mother, 'You'll be pleased to know, Mrs

Morris. Nothing wrong with him.

One time as we came away from the clinic she gave me a right shake. 'Nothing wrong with you. Nothing wrong with you. They don't know the half of it. Bed-wetting at ten years old. Can't hold a knife or fork the right way. Can't tell the time. Can't read. Can't write. There's something wrong with you all right. They just haven't got a name for it. Pain in the bloody arse, that's what I'd call it. And, whatever it is, we know whose side it came from.'

I move down the main path towards the entrance. I want to see if the gate is now locked up as they said. Perhaps the smallpox story is true and the council want to keep people out when they start digging up the bodies. I should have paid more attention to the conversation earlier. Their talk of a night-watchman. Before I know it I'm almost on top of his little stripey hut.

And there's a dog. Black, and barking like crazy.

And now I am running. As hard as I can. Never outpace this brute. My runty little legs won't move fast enough. All that junk food and sitting in front of the telly.

Yet . . . I know which direction to take. Where to go. Know where the animal would not, could not, follow me. I scramble the last few paces and jump up onto my part of the dyke. Looking down I see the dog; its eyes gleam red in the dark night. Its forepaws scrabble at the wall. I pull my feet up. It steps back to prepare itself to spring, its feet among the white ash. Then it stops and is strangely silent. It lifts its paws, one by one, shaking them hopelessly. Then it starts to whine, a high-pitched noise with little frantic yipping barks. It retreats rapidly, stops, then, lifting its head to the sky, it howls.

I'll never forget that. All the hair on its back rose and stood upright on its neck and shoulders, as the dog moved slowly backwards baying to the heavens. The moon showed briefly in the troubled sky. The animal paused, then turned and fled.

It's terribly cold. I'm shaking so hard my legs can hardly hold me. I nearly topple from the wall into the hole where the tree's roots are lying naked to the sky.

I'm not staying here. Down the other side and off through the wood. I'll go the long way home.

Sometimes we get a night frost in late spring, we're so far north. But this cold is different. It's like a house that hasn't been lived in for years.

An utter absence of heat.

Deep intense chill.

A tomb.

Chapter 7

It's almost midnight when I get home. He's flaked out on the couch, mouth open. The telly's talking loudly to itself. I pause before drawing the curtains over.

The world news. Images of starving children and warring adults are reflected on my window panes. The lights in the street beyond and the houses opposite are ghostly shadows. Are the pictures which I see captured on the glass a distortion or for real? I shut the blinds and they disappear.

When I was younger I thought that the people on the telly were actually there. Then at night when the set was turned off, they got smaller and smaller, and slid down the cables all the way to London or wherever. In Primary Five the teacher explained to the class how television actually worked. I remember thinking that my idea was more sensible.

I try not to look at him lying there like a felled tree, jaw slack, face worn and stubbly. I throw a travelling rug over him and go through to the kitchen.

I just leave the mess. I don't have the energy to clear up this war zone. I find some bread and make a sandwich and go upstairs.

As I take my jeans off I find the notice which I took from the graveyard earlier. I spread out the crumpled paper on the floor and peer at it closely.

"NOTICE OF INTENT."
"Intimation of intention by the District Council to exhume the entire contents of Stone Mill Burial Graveyard and re-inter the remains elsewhere."

I squint at it with one eye closed. Sometimes that helps. Or if I cover up most of the print and try it one word at a time.

> "Town and Country Planning (Churches, Places of Religious Worship and Burial Grounds) (Scotland) Regulations 1948. Provision of inspection of Register of Burials."

It's too difficult for me to work out exactly what it says. I've had a problem with print for as long as I can remember. From the very first reading book I ever had.

'Don't worry. It'll come,' Dad would ruffle my hair as I stumbled over each set of black symbols. Then he'd take the book from me and start to read. Giving it all the actions, and voices, and making faces, his story was always so much better . . .

Even she couldn't stop laughing. Sometimes.

'You're not helping him,' she'd say, moaning on again.

'What do those teachers know?' he'd say. 'Nothing. Not living in the real world, most of them.' And he would wink at me behind her back, and we were pals together.

And it was as if there were coloured lights in my head. Silver and gold. I rode with princes and chased dragons. I crept with Mowgli in the jungle and peered out from behind the deep green leaves, my heart thudding in excitement.

I look at the typed notice again. Why doesn't it work for me? Now I just pretend that it does. There's a dozen different tricks to avoid getting caught. You watch, copy, listen, and repeat what someone else says. Ask to leave the classroom before it gets to your turn to read out. Cause a disturbance, get sent out. Cheat.

I stuff it in my rucksack. I'll get Peter to look at it in school tomorrow. I need to tell him what happened tonight. I don't really understand it myself. Maybe I've imagined more than I saw. I was tired and cold and hungry. My arm aches badly where I caught it on the tree. I pull up my sleeve.

There is a pinkish rash around the cut. I slosh some water on it and go to bed.

I suppose I was scratching it, and that's why it became sore and itchy, and why I was restless that night. And you never do sleep peacefully if something's bothering you.

Perhaps it was in my mind what the professor had said about smallpox. Blisters and scabs on your skin.

Or maybe it was because something had already started to happen. Something which could not be stopped. Reaching out, seeking contact, searching for a way through. Whatever reason.

That night I have the first terrible dream.

At first it was the trees. In the small wood behind the kirkyard where I was walking. The branches on the bushes, brushing across my face, snatching at my sleeve, tearing my skin. Then the trailing leaves, rustling, rustling, as I moved among them. So I stride more quickly, increase my pace as I march along, but they try to trip me up and pull me back. Then in the aisles between the tombs. Great creepers are trailing like serpents, stone vine tendrils winding round my ankles. I shake them from me, lifting each foot, one by one by one.

And the voices whispering. Closely. By my ear. When I turn my head, they move too. Quickly. Just out of reach.

The tombstone with the urn beckons me. Dark grey cloth cascading from its stone vase, billowing in a breeze which is not there. Falling across my face. First, softly, gently. Then as I raise my hand to brush it away, insistently it swathes my face, my arms, now it's wrapped around my neck, vast folds of dark material. And the voices, no, it's one voice, muttering, muttering. The musty dank smell is in my nostrils, in my mouth. I struggle and the winding sheet stretches tighter, pulling me down, choking my life away.

I leap up in bed with a loud cry. I look about me. What is that in the corner of my room? In deep shadows, whispering, whispering, whispering in my head? But . . . it is the sound of rain battering on my window. That's what woke me up. Isn't it?

Isn't it?

And I've been caught up too tightly in my bed covers. That explains it. Doesn't it?

I get up.

My head aches with a half-remembered fear. Something important throbs in my skull. Something I should do. To look for. I cannot recall what it is. There is a compulsion pulling me one way. To do what? Go where? Yet behind that is a fainter shadow telling me something different. Don't go. Don't touch it. Don't go.

Outside the sky is pitted and pock-marked. The cherry blossom flowers will be scattered in the cemetery, driven down, pink and white among the red gravel.

It's nearly a quarter to nine. I'm late. But I have to get to school. Too many absences mean snooping social workers and "place of safety" orders. A while ago, when she first left and he "wasn't coping", I spent a few months in a children's home. No way am I going back there.

I wash my face and, to fend off the BO, I turn my tee shirt inside out. I find an almost clean pair of socks. They don't match exactly, but then under my boots, no one will notice.

I completely forget Tuesday is a PE day.

Chapter 8

'Forgotten your kit again?' sneers Watkins. He picks up a pair of shorts from the lost property box in the changing rooms and throws them at me.

'Here, put these on, and take those heavy boots off.'

I run out into the hall. The others are already lined up.

'How old are you, boy?' yells Watkins. 'Old enough to dress yourself, I would have thought,' he goes on without waiting for a reply.

Old and cold and bold and sold.

He walks up behind me and flicks my ear. 'So. Why do we have our tee shirt on outside in?'

Flick. Flick. Flick.

'And our socks are odd.'

Flick. Flick. Flick.

'Did we know that?'

Actually, yes.

'But then, you are an odd little sod altogether,' he mutters under his breath. He sniffs the air. 'And a bit whiffy too,' he says loudly. He marches down the hall, arms swinging, thick thighs mottled red.

'Right. From the top. Run up to the springboard, one forward roll on top of the box, climb the wallbars, jump down and jog a circuit.'

I can't do it. Never could. I have been skipping PE since we first came into his class last August. If I'd remembered this morning that we were having PE today I would have stayed off. The last time I tried to do this exercise I nearly broke my neck. I look around desperately. The line is moving quickly forward. I can feel my insides melting. It's my turn.

34

He's standing waiting beside the springboard. 'Come on, Solly boy. I'll help you over.'

I start a run in.

'STOP!' He holds up his hand and steps out in front of me. 'Go back and start again. And this time act as though you intend to go across.'

The rest of the class have slowed down. They are watching. Most of them know I can't co-ordinate. After all, they've seen my progress since Primary One. Or, in fact, haven't.

I get ready. I see his sneer. I decide that this time I'm not stopping. I put my head down and charge.

Maybe I slipped to the side or something, although I'm sure he stepped forward as well. Probably to push me over. I rebound against his chest and we're both on the floor. There are whoops and catcalls from the audience. I'm on my feet before he is. I meet his gaze as he gets up slowly.

'We've got ways of dealing with your sort,' he says softly. There are small collections of spit at each side of his mouth.

'Sorry, sir. It was an accident.'

'Of course it was,' he says, 'of course it was.' He calls over a couple of boys. 'Put this equipment away. I think we'll have a quick game of fives.'

He plays opposite me. It was just a case of when it was coming.

Not long to wait.

Fouled in front of the goal. Tripped at the halfway line. Bumping and barging. I decide I've had enough.

'Sir, I need the lav.'

'No, you don't.'

'I do.'

I turn to go. The ball hits me with force on the face. I stumble. He comes across.

'Sorry, Sol. It was an accident.'

I see him through a blur. My head is thumping. I wipe my face on my sleeve, and taste salty tears. I have to get away.

'Hang about, you,' Watkins shouts at me. 'A little knock

and you scuttle off. Time to grow up.' His voice is higher than usual. He comes towards me. 'We can't have you running away, like a namby-pamby.' He waves play on.

'I'm going off,' I say.

Nobody moves.

'I'm going off,' he mimics me.

He's standing right in front of me. I can see hairs sprouting from his nostrils. If I could get the first one in quick, I could burst his nose. Leave a mark. He studies me. Rocks on his heels. Smiling.

'Sol, don't,' says Peter. He lays his hand gently on my arm. I unclench my fist slowly, slowly.

Watkins is livid. He turns to Peter, but before he can say anything Peter holds up a broken lace.

'Lace snapped, sir. Can I get another one?'

He's clever, Peter.

Watkins' eyes refocus. He stares at me for a second.

'Go and stand in the corridor. And this time don't run off home to mummy.'

There's a group of infants in the passage waiting to use the games hall. The teacher stares at me.

'Are you in Mr Watkins' class?'

I nod, fingering my bruise. She tuts, and puts her hand to my face. Cool hand with crimson fingernails.

Watkins is at the door. 'Mzzzzz Talmur,' he oils. 'May I introduce you to one of my star pupils? Solomon Morris.'

He turns to me. 'Sol, sonny. This is our new member of staff. She takes Primary One. You'll have a lot in common,' he adds and smirks.

Ms Talmur tilts her head up and stares Watkins down. Then she turns to me. 'I'm very pleased to meet you, Solomon,' she says. And she gives me her hand.

I'm so stunned that I shake it. She smiles firmly and doesn't let go until I look at her.

'You've had an . . . accident?' She hesitates over the word and turns to Watkins. 'Solomon seems to have hurt himself.'

'Yes, dear. Boys usually do have a bit of rough and tumble in the gym hall.'

'Do they?' she asks, all fluffy and light. 'I grew up with six older brothers. Any "rough and tumble" which ended like that usually meant that someone was doing a bit of bullying.'

Crack.

He doesn't know what to do. I chance another look from under my puffy eyelid. She's shepherding her little class through the door.

'Come along, take hands. Someone show Amy where to go. She's new.'

They're gone. He's trembling. So am I. I lean against the wall and make with the blank I'm-not-here-at-all face of a ghetto inmate.

'Bitch!'

He notices me.

'Right. I'll sort that. You, sunshine, are relegated. You are going to spend the rest of the day in the Primary One class.'

Chapter 9

The chairs and tables are much smaller than I remember. Everything else is the same.

The smell. Chalk. Stale milk. Pee.

The walls. Splurges of colours. Custard yellow, pillar-box red, frightening green. Samples of crabbed writing and elongated scrawling.

On the windowsills trays of bright beads and blocks. In the corner the dressing-up box . . . .

I had loved that. Opening the huge wicker hamper, the lid creaking as it fell back. The jumble of coloured cloth. Taking out the pieces of material to choose from, stroking fur and silk, the feel of crushed velvet and crisp lace. Trying on hats and helmets, cloaks and coats.

You could be anything you wanted to be. Any other person. Real or imagined. It's one of the times I can recall when I was happy in school. Being someone else.

There are drawings pinned up on the walls. Fat circle faces, with huge curvy grins on them, and all around the outside edge, coils of hair like a crazy clockmaker's springs.

My circles were never round. I made them the wrong way. At least that's what old Mrs Webber used to say. Everybody else drew theirs anti-clockwise, mine went from right to left, and ended up squint. I had Mrs Webber for the first four years. I think I probably loved her. She was a round plump little lady. Warm and soft and cuddly, and I got to sit right by her when she told the class a story.

She called me her special boy.

Now I know.

For "special" read "stupid".

None of my shapes were right, not the circles or the squares, letters or numbers, lines, curved or straight. I even wrote some of them backwards. Fives and threes and eights were indistinguishable.

Are.

It took ages before I realised that those lines on the pages of books matched up with spoken words. Flat and boring, black on white, the little clumps of letters couldn't be connected to the sounds which formed the pictures in my head. I didn't even need the illustrations. I could see Jason's sword in his hand and feel the hot breath of the hydra on my face. And at night I told them back to my dad, every sentence complete.

Then Mrs Webber would ask me to point to a word on the page.

And I couldn't.

I heard her talking to my mother one day. 'Don't worry. He's probably a late developer. He'll improve as he gets older. Just wait and you'll see.'

Only my mum hadn't. Waited around long enough that is, to find out.

I always sat in the same seat. Number four.

I sit down now. My legs stick out into the passage. The door opens and Ms Talmur comes in, the children in twos behind her. She doesn't miss a step.

'Ah, Solomon,' she says. 'I was told I might expect someone to . . . help me this afternoon. I didn't realise it would be you.'

Oh, yeah?

'Children, go into your groups. Amy, you haven't got a group yet. Sit with Solomon just now until I sort things out.' She starts to organise the class as the one called Amy climbs onto the chair beside me.

I look at her. Her pretty face and red-brown curls. She smiles. She has two teeth missing at the front. I look away.

'Good.' Ms Talmur is at the desk, 'I'm glad to see you have

39

made friends. Solomon, would you take out your jotter and get on with a bit of free writing while I prepare some material for Amy? She has just moved here. Her dad is supervising the moving of the stones in the old kirkyard.'

What?

'Come on, Amy.' She takes the child's hand.

I take my jotter out and lean over to one side and across the desk. I curve my arm round and tuck the jotter into the crook of my arm. I start to write. Slowly.

'Solomon, if you're left-handed then you might find it easier to place your jotter like this.' Ms Talmur leans over me. She adjusts my position so that I'm not covering my work as I write.

There is a musky scented smell from her as her face bends close to mine, a warm closeness that makes me want to touch her. Then I see her mouth turn down as she looks at my writing. She flicks back through the pages. She sees the red pen corrections, pages and pages of them. My hands start to sweat.

She is reading some of my work. Her lips move, the scarlet outlines changing shape as she mouths the sounds.

She says something.

I don't hear it.

I've blocked her out. I know what's coming next. Been through this routine a dozen times or more. Could write the script for her – if I could write, that is.

She stretches over and takes a book from the corner bookcase. She places it down flat in front of me.

'Can you read that title?'

It has a picture of the ugly duckling on the front.

'*The Ugly Duckling*,' I say calmly. 'By Hans Christian Andersen,' I add.

Nice touch, that.

I look directly at her.

'Would you read something from that book for me, please?' she asks.

'Sure,' I say. I turn the pages casually, find a place and read her a sentence or two.

A wrinkle appears on her forehead. She's not convinced. I lean over and take a few more books. I open them at different pages and read the sentences out loud. She smiles at me.

'Clever boy,' she says softly. She examines the books carefully, lifts her eyes and looks round the room. 'Clever Solomon. But how are you doing it?'

'Dunno what you mean, miss.'

'Oh, yes, you do.' She chews her lip, thinking hard. 'You had Mrs Webber didn't you? All the way up the school. Did you sit at the same table every year, say this one, the fourth seat? She would take the reading round the class in the exact same order each morning, so all you had to do was get someone to read you the fourth sentence and then memorise it.'

There is a trickle of sweat running down between my shoulder blades. *No one*, not even Peter, has ever worked out how I coped with reading aloud.

'Dunno what you mean, miss.'

She partly covers her mouth with her hand and, turning her head away, she says something.

'What?'

She looks back to me. Eyes grey-green. 'So there's nothing amiss with your hearing.'

I can't go through all this again.

'Hang on a moment, please,' she says. She goes into a store cupboard and comes out a moment later with a pack of cards and a plastic tray.

'Would you look at them for me, please, Solomon?'

It's going to be the same old routine. And I'd thought she might have been different.

Now they are in front of me. Spread out like a torturer's implements. Cards laid out on the tray, various shapes picked out in different coloured dots. Her nails are tap, tap, tapping on the pale wood of the desk. My head is aching now and the coloured dots tremble and merge, swimming across the page.

'Don't think of them as alphabet letters, or try to tell me what they are. Just trace the outline of what you can see.'

I put my head down.

'Draw that shape for me. There.' She points with her long red finger nails among the blue and green and orange dots.

Green sludgy green.

Blood orange red.

Red alert.

Her tray is slippy in my hands as I lift it and chuck it against the wall. I bang my fists on the table and stand up; the table comes with me. I turn and kick myself free of it and the chair. I run round and pull down the boxes from the window ledges. The lego pieces and the coloured straws scatter before me.

I bite the sleeve of my jumper. I can hear the ripping cloth. I whirl round.

There is something there in her eyes. Cloudy, shades of a sea storm. Pity? I take her handbag and empty it out onto her desk, then I hurl it at the blackboard. I grab some of the contents of her bag. Her personal things. Mirror, lipstick, comb. I smash them on the floor.

Her eyes are sharper now, bright with fear. And I am glad. It makes me stronger, exultant.

I wrench the classroom door open. I'm free. I'm running down the corridor, screaming.

Chapter 10

I am not alone.

On my wall, in the dark, wrapped in my blanket, I wait for dawn. Nowhere else to go. Think in the morning I'll steal some money somewhere and take off for London or up north.

And now, in this place beside my poor raped rowan tree, I know that I am not alone. Its body is lying crushed on the ground. Its leaves have withered quickly. The little creamy white flowers will now never produce their fruit. They're brownish yellow and dying on the surface of the earth. As if a pestilence has struck them.

Upset and turbulence all around this place where I used to feel safe. More soil has been taken from the base of the tree. The hole is deeper and wider but the roots seem to spread out and run deep. Like a wart I once cut around and tried to take from my finger. Its sinewy white tentacles had groped down into my flesh.

They have been removing quantities of earth to dig it out. The air itself is full of unrest. I cannot sleep.

And now. Whispers in the wind.

I sit up quickly. There are two voices. That became important later. After the "accident" I was unclear about things. Fear does that. Freezes your brain. Real terror, scattering your reason. But I know that in the beginning there were two of them. I heard them talking.

'This way, Gerry. I left the shovels here.'

I roll over in my hiding place and look down into the old churchyard. Two figures are among the diggings. Two figures creeping about.

Why?

I manoeuvre myself onto my stomach and watch.

'Hold the torch and I'll clear the earth.'

'Hope this is worth the effort, Joe.' The smaller one, who is wearing some kind of brown workman's overalls, is holding the torch. His hand shakes and the light wavers. 'Gives me the creeps being here at night.'

They were at the wall directly below me.

'I'm telling you now. There's something worth money down there. What else would be in a chest fastened up like that? If we leave it one more day Frame will notice that this tree is taking too long to uproot. He'll be over to find out why. You listen to me. The officials find it first and it'll end up in a museum. We dig it out tonight, no one knows but us, and we get to keep what's there.'

I can hear their grunts as they shovel out the earth. A faint breeze ruffles my hair.

The sound of metal striking metal.

'Got it! Give's a hand here, Ger.'

The moon speeds out from behind the clouds and I see them grappling a heavy lidded chest out of the hole.

'God! It's well done up. Locked and bolted and chained. Whoever put this away wanted to make sure no one got into it.'

Or out.

Joe laughs. 'Good job I brought a crowbar.'

He fits it through a hasp and levers. Both of them so intent on what they are doing that at first they are not aware of the ground around them shifting slowly. I feel the wall beneath me tremble.

'CURSE!' There's an almighty crack and the one called Joe swears loudly.

'I don't believe it,' he says. 'The bloody crowbar's snapped.'

'Eh, you're bleeding, Joe,' says his mate. 'Look.'

'Yeah, it's nothing. I'll see to it in a minute. Mind yourself now, this earth's so soggy with the rain we'll be up to our

44

ankles in a minute.'

There's blood coming from the wound on his wrist. Blood dripping onto the iron chest. I watch the warm dark liquid trickling down through the hinges.

'Well, at least we've got it undone.'

He's right. One of the hasps has broken and the lid is very slightly askew.

'Let's see what's in there.' He reaches into the opening.

Suddenly I feel the earth itself vibrate. Loose stones fall from the wall. There's a great groaning sound and the torch light goes out.

'Holy Mary! What was that?'

Nothing.

No sound. No movement. No breath of wind. A nothingness that reaches out into your mind. I shake my head.

'No,' I cry. But to whom, to what?

'Joe?' Gerry swings the torch about.

It's as if the sides of the hole have collapsed back in on themselves, taking the box with them. But where is Joe? The light from the torch is shaking violently.

'Joe? Joe, where are you?' Gerry moves forward to look down into the earth. There isn't any room for him to be under the metal chest. Can't be. Where has he gone?

'Stop fooling about.' Gerry casts around him with the torch. He laughs, or tries to. 'Come on out of it.'

In the beam of the light I can still see the top of the box, the hasp broken, the lid to one side. Is there something moving inside?

The nothing feeling is stronger. The coldness complete. As the void left by a fallen star or the emptiness of despair.

'Whatyesay?' Gerry mutters something and steps towards the box.

Then I act. The faint shadow in my dream of last night is sharper, clearer. I have to stop the other man touching that chest. I don't mean to give away my hiding place. It's a stupid thing to do. I just remember having an absolute conviction that if Joe was in the grave he was not coming out again. Not ever.

'Don't,' I cry.

'Almighty God.' Gerry screams as he turns and sees my white face hovering above him in the moonlight. He runs.

I jump down. There is a sense of power coming from the earth. From this part of the cemetery in which nothing grows. I look about me. Empty silence chokes the night. There is no one there.

Yet . . . .

It's as if there are others with me. I am among folk I know. Pals. I can hear them laughing and chatting just out of reach, calling to me, friendly-like. They want me to join them.

All I need to do is to reach out to them.

Reach down.

Inside the chest.

I lift my arm. I turn my head. I am alone. Myself. Something moves in my mind. I am alone.

I repeat the phrase aloud. 'I am alone,' I say.

But I'm not. There's my father's laughter in the air. His great ringing shout; he has started a story and I must hear the end. With the smell of warm toast and the taste of melted butter in my mouth.

And it's there for the taking. Just for me, if I want it.

And I do. All I have to do is . . . stretch out my hand.

I reach out my hand.

Chapter 11

'LIES.'

The sound hissed in my ear.

Lies. Lies. Lies.

Was there a word written on the chest? Dead leaves from the rowan tree had fallen on the lid. They rustled, disturbed by a small whisper of air. Was that what I heard?

No, there *was* lettering. Their moving had revealed it on the lid. "HERE LYE . . ."

A brief moment, a break in the cloud, allows the moonlight to shine down on me crouched in the earth, and into the disturbed grave.

"HERE LYE THE ASHES OF . . . . MALEFICE"

I mouth out the words . . . M-A-L-E-F-I-C-E . . . and suddenly it is cold in the kirkyard, very cold. Black shadows gyrate across the space between my hand and the dark metal. My fingers stop. I hesitate. There is a wind amongst the yew trees, a wind that snuffles and moans between the branches. I know I am not alone. I look around me. I see only tall tombstones huddled like conspirators in the darkness.

A cold grey light is pouring into the churchyard. Dawn, edging out blackness, as the planet spins away from the night. And suddenly my urge to reach down into the grave is gone.

I move my head and it is as if space shifts. I lean back on my heels. The town clock strikes the hour and time flows back again like a river around me. I shiver and stand up. As I do so the earth I am standing on slides suddenly, tumbles and falls in from the sides of the hole. I step back quickly to stop being pulled in. The sods thud back and cover the chest. I move away and as I do so my foot catches a small object shining in the grass. A ring. I pick it up and put it in my back pocket. I collect my blanket from the ledge and stuff it in my rucksack. I'm never going to sleep there again.

It is only when I am out in the main road that I hear the call of a bird's morning song.

There is something weird going on, something unexplained. Whatever is in that chest is wrong in some way, yet I had been about to open it up. Why? Every instinct had told me not to . . . yet I had felt compelled to reach out and touch . . . What?

Two nights of disturbed sleep aren't helping me to think very clearly. Where was the first workman? The one his friend called Joe? He must have run off when the box fell back into the hole.

The whine of the milk float gently teases my brain back to normality. The gun-metal grey of the sky has charred patches of rain cloud on it. The milkman nods to me and it. 'Rain before breakfast at this rate,' he says.

I open our back door very slowly. One of the panes of glass has been broken and a piece of cardboard wedged in the frame. Various pieces of crockery lie on the floor and the contents of the cupboards remain strewn all over the worktops. He is sitting at the kitchen table, red-eyed and unshaven, a mug of coffee in front of him. His hands shake as he drinks it.

'Sorry, son. A million times.'

I walk past him. No wonder she left.

I sit down on my bed and drop the rucksack on the floor. My head hurts so much. I can't go to school. There will be a major investigation into yesterday's trouble. But if I stay off again, someone might come round. That could be worse. The state he's in, and the way the house is wrecked, every social worker in the area would be drafted in to deal with us. There was no telling either whether he would start drinking again. It sometimes happened that way. He would ricochet from bender to bender until like a spent bullet he ran out of force. Then he would lie in bed for days, crushed and useless.

A hesitant knock on the door. I get up and open it. He's standing there with a tray. I look at it. Cup of coffee, plate of toast. I strike it out of his hand onto the floor. He doesn't say anything, just gets down on his hands and knees to clear up the mess.

I slam my bedroom door and wedge a chair against it, noisily, so that he will hear me doing it.

I lie down on my bed and stare at my ceiling. There are posters and magazine cut-outs pinned up. Gandalf the Grey. Elves and goblins. He had drawn some of them for me. Great swathes of colour sweeping across my room. Palaces floating on shining lakes, crystal waterfalls gushing from magic mountains. Fantasy.

Something in my jeans pocket jabs into my side. I pull out the ring I had picked up earlier. I turn it in my hand. It is gold, broad and heavy. Maybe I'll get something for it from one of the traders at the market on Saturday.

'Blast.' There's writing engraved inside. That'll take the value down. I squint at it and try to read it slowly. What does it say?

A name, I think. Then a word. I spell out F-O-R-E-V-E-R. Then another name. There are numbers too, as part of the inscription. I can't work it out. It's too complex. Why don't they make capital letters the same shape as small ones, and just have it that you have to write them bigger? It would make things much easier.

Suddenly I have a thought. Maybe the ring came from the chest. Maybe the first workman had picked it out before the box slipped away from him. He had known there were things worth having buried there. If I could get back before they did, then I could make some money out of this. What had been written on the lid? "Malefice."

I would have to find out what that meant.

A tapping on my bedroom door. I stuff the ring back in my pocket.

My father's speaking. 'There's someone from the school downstairs. I said you were sick but they won't go away. Said they had to see you.'

Chapter 12

It was her. Ms Talmur, standing like a trapped butterfly in our dingy hallway. My father beside her, unshaven, in grubby clothes.

What was she thinking? Seeing the stained wall paper, the worn carpet, the broken handle on the living room door?

It doesn't seem to bother her. She looks around her casually and then straight at me coming down the stairs.

'Ah, Solomon, there you are. If you get your school bag I'll give you a lift to school this morning.'

It's an order.

'I'm going to ask the Head if you can help me out today,' she says as we get into her car. 'The parents of the new pupil intake for next term are visiting and I could use some assistance.'

'I need to go to my class.' I stare out of the window at the rain.

'No, you don't,' she says firmly. 'You probably hate your class.'

What's it to you?

She changes gear. 'I didn't report the incident yesterday.'

I shrug. 'Don't care if you do.'

She sighs. 'No, you probably don't,' she says.

We were crossing the old bridge, the river rushing below, swollen with flood water.

'Look, truthfully, I actually *do* need some assistance with the programme I've got planned for today, and I would like you to help me.'

'Why? Why me?' This time *I* stare at her.

She blinks.

Now, here comes the lie.

"Very clever with his hands, Solomon is, handy to have about if you want some furniture moved, well, large pieces anyway." (He must be good at something, surely.)

'Actually, because I don't know anyone else in the school,' she says. 'Also, I think you're the type of pupil that teachers don't want in their class. So, if I ask leave for you to come and not someone else, they'll probably say yes.'

Well, that was the truth and a half.

She grins at me, white teeth and red lips. I give a kind of laugh. Couldn't help it.

So, I'm in the assembly hall. And she's right, she does need help. This is going to be the most amazing parent introduction to the infant school ever. The janny and I have been hauling benches and chairs and tables and boxes of stuff around all morning.

'New notions, never had to do this before,' he's grumbling and swearing away. 'Old Mrs Webber just gave everybody a wee talk and a cup of tea. That's all that was needed. Still is, if you ask me. *And*, it'll all have to go back again afterwards.'

'Nearly finished.' She's all smiles and charm. 'Thank you *so* much, Mr Grimbley. We could never have managed without you, could we, Solomon?'

I shrug and look away.

Don't get close. Don't stand so. Stand so, close to me.

She has noticed me scratching my arm.

'Let me see.' She draws back the sleeve of my jumper and draws her breath in. 'What happened?'

'Fell out a tree.'

I don't like the look of my skin. It's red and weeping where the branch cut through. She takes me to the medical room and cleans it out with antiseptic cream.

'There,' she says briskly. 'That will sort you out.' She winks at me. 'I have special healing powers, being the seventh child of a seventh child. Now we'll go and have some lunch. The parents are arriving at one-thirty.'

This should be good.

They arrive and she makes with the intro. First all the boring stuff about emergency contacts, special diets, reading schemes, blah, blah. Some have heard it all before. Second child. Can't really spare the time away from the office. Hope she hurries up. Got to get back. Waiting for an important fax. One business suit keeps checking his watch.

Others . . . well, it's their first, and it's all new and exciting and they want the very very best for Nigel, who can actually read already, and does have his own set of Encyclopaedia Britannica.

And . . . I have this really strange sensation. I'm sitting on the stairs at the side of the stage, and this quiet glow starts inside of me. Sometimes, at home, when he's been OK for a bit, we get a video for the weekend and he cooks some dinner. Then, just before we sit down I have this feeling same as I've got now. Like I know that something interesting is going to happen, something pleasant, and for a space around me, everything is going to be all right. A small peace to swim into, a patch of sun to sit in, a bit of time that excludes the rest.

When did it start to be this way with me? Are other peoples' lives the same, with only little hiccups of happiness in amongst the misery?

Ms Talmur has finished her preliminaries. 'Now . . .' she says. 'All those parents who will have children in my class next term, I would like you to pay particular attention. This is what I would like you to do.

'Now the fun begins,' she says under her breath.

I feel I should warn her. 'If they try to sit on those chairs at the back they will fall over,' I say.

'Exactly,' she says smugly. 'How often does that happen to an infant? And when it does, people laugh, or clap their hands and tell them to get up quickly. Don't they?' She rubs her hands together and gives me a big grin. 'And that's just what we are going to do to them.'

They really didn't know what to expect, those parents.

'I would like all of you to complete a very simple exercise before leaving the school today. Something that your children will be asked to do every day of their life.' She points to the tables set behind her. 'I am going to ask each one of you to come out and put on a school tie,' she pauses, 'after having first put on a pair of gloves.'

'This is ridiculous,' grumbles one man. I recognise him. He owns the fast food takeaway on the main street. He's really overweight, gross. His stomach wobbles as he sits on the ordinary stacking chair. He's never going to manage the obstacle course we've constructed at the other end of the hall.

She ignores him.

'After which I would like you all to choose a coloured crayon from the box.' She points to the box which we've set on top of a pair of step-ladders and is practically impossible to reach into. 'Then go to your desk at the back of the hall, and draw me a picture.'

There are some murmurs of enquiry from her audience. A few of them are shaking their heads. She smiles at them cheerfully. 'Perhaps I'd better explain why.'

Chapter 13

Ms Talmur claps her hands loudly and starts to speak.

'I would like you to humour me for the next half hour or so and take part in this programme which I have designed to help you understand your children better. If anyone feels that they do not wish to do this then I would ask them to leave now. But if you stay, then you must remain for the whole of the session. In fact,' she gives them all one of her best smiles, 'I'll take it as a sign of failure if you tell me that you want to leave.'

They settle down a bit then, and they all nod. Every one of them.

'Good. What we are going to do now is to imagine that you are the children who make up the new intake into this school. All right?' She smiles grimly. 'Most of us have forgotten what it is like to be four or five and exist in a world inhabited by giants.' She covers her eyes with her fingers. 'Close your eyes and imagine what it would be like to live with no income, no status, no rights. How it would feel to be small and completely powerless. That is what your children have to contend with each day of their lives. For one short afternoon you are going to re-experience this.'

They close their eyes. Most of them are smiling.

'Thank you,' says Ms Talmur. 'You may open your eyes again, but from now on I have complete control over you, your minds and bodies. My word is law.'

Her voice has developed a nasty edge. There is a strangely sinister undertone present, a mild, unstated but very real threat implied.

'I want you to come out here, one by one, and put on these

gloves.' Her voice has changed again. She is speaking to them in that irritating, sing-song way that some teachers use when they address small children. She walks along the rows of chairs where they are sitting, patting one or two on the head as she does so.

'All right,' she pushes her face right up close to the first parent at the end of the line. 'What's YOUR name?'

'Mr Gordon,' he says.

'Your first name, son,' she says.

'John.'

'JOHN,' she yells. 'That's a LOVELY name. Isn't it, class?'

They all agree, a few of them smiling.

'My goodness, we are not very polite boys and girls, are we? We should really say, "Yes, Ms Talmur." Shall we try that again?'

'Yes, Ms Talmur.' There is a scattered response.

'All together, please.'

'Yes, Ms Talmur.'

'I didn't hear you,' she says sweetly. 'I said, that's a LOVELY name, isn't it, class?'

'Yes, Ms Talmur,' they all chorused.

They were enjoying themselves.

So far.

'Well, John,' she says loudly, dragging him to his feet. 'You can be the very first good boy to come out and put your gloves on. Go on.' She gives him a hard push. 'Ooops, clumsy you,' she laughs, as he stumbles slightly.

'Next,' she smiles a brittle smile.

'Jean Malcolm,' the next victim speaks up.

'Stand up and tell all the class,' says Ms Talmur, 'and do fix your dress, pet.' She leans over and hauls at this woman's very smart clothes to straighten out a non-existent crease.

'Jea—'

'Off you go,' Ms Talmur interrupts her testily. 'You're holding up the line, dear.'

Out they come, one by one, saying their names and then going forward to put on the assortment of gloves laid out on the tables in front of them. Boxing gloves, ski mitts, outsize rubber gloves with cotton wool stuffed down the fingers and several mis-matched gardening and working gloves.

'Now, each of you pick up a tie from the pile and put it on,' she instructs them.

'Oh, do hurry up, Mary-Anne,' she says crossly to one lady. 'And you,' she turns on someone who is laughing, 'surely a big boy like you can tie your own tie.'

The results are hilarious.

'Now, pick a crayon and find your desk and do your very best drawing for me.'

They fumble about in the crayon box. One parent decided to take an active part. He holds up a broken piece of blue crayon.

'Please, Miss, this is broken,' he says, 'and I want a green one.'

'Go and stand in the corner,' she tells him at once. 'And face the wall. We don't like greedy children in this school. I'll deal with you later.'

The tables and chairs are at the back of the hall. The janny and I have placed them on top of stacked benches.

'You mean we have to climb up on to that to reach our seats?' asks the fat man.

'You must put up your hand if you want to speak in class,' she says. 'I don't want to have to tell Mummy and Daddy that you have been a rude little boy, do I?' she asks him sweetly.

He puts his hand up. 'Where do I sit?' he asks.

'Find your own desks,' she instructs them.

I stand up to watch this bit. She has stickered the tables with names. They are written backwards, upside down, letters wrong way round, some just squiggles.

'This is impossible,' snaps one lady. I recognise her. She is a receptionist at the health clinic, unhelpful and superior.

'Now, Gertrude,' says Ms Talmur, very patronising, 'don't tell me a smart girl like you can't read her own name?' She walks away from her before she can answer.

'Look, this is impossible,' says brown business suit. 'You have to help us.'

'Ah,' says Ms Talmur. 'You need help. Why don't you ask?'

'Would you help me find my seat, teacher?' he asks, humouring her.

She puts her hand behind her ear. 'And what's the magic word?'

'Please,' he grits his teeth.

'Good boy,' she reaches up and pats his cheek.

She marches around the room, pausing now and then to tick off someone. She deals out her pack of cards, little humiliations, small put-downs; she uses a whole arsenal of negative remarks.

And they have no option but to accept them and play with the hand they're given. Using a gratingly loud pitch, her words and manner are calculated to annoy. Condescending remarks sting like insect bites.

'We ARE a bit of a crosspatch this morning.'

'Who's a Bad Mood Bear then?'

'Isn't this fun?' she whispers as she passes me. And it is.

She stops beside one man who is still trying to fix his tie. 'Do you need the lavatory, William?'

'No.'

'Yes, you do,' she insists. 'You've been fiddling about with your clothes for some time now.'

'No,' he gasps.

'Yes, you have. And if you can't do yourself up get one of the bigger boys to help you. Off you go,' she propels him out the door.

Brown business suit is the first to break. His stool tips over and he lands on his bum on the floor. 'Your game isn't very funny,' he yells, struggling to get up.

58

'It's not meant to be funny,' she says calmly. She stands back and watches him scrambling to his feet. She doesn't offer assistance. 'And it is NOT a game.'

She lifts her head and addresses all of them. 'These are the circumstances, to a greater or lesser degree, in which your children have to live their lives. When your child behaves badly or is scared, upset, lonely or frightened, you might want to recall what your emotions are at this moment. If they display bad temper, bed-wet or don't do as well in school as you want or expect them to, then try to remember how you felt today.'

They shuffle out. I have a feeling that some might complain to the headteacher. She doesn't seem to be too bothered. She is humming happily away as we gather up the stuff.

'What did you think of that, then, Solomon?' she asks me.

I start to reply when the door opens abruptly and Professor Miller hurries in.

'Ms Talmur,' he says, 'I'm extremely anxious about Amy. We can't seem to find her anywhere in the school.'

Chapter 14

'Perhaps I missed her in the corridor.' Professor Miller turns round quickly and hurries back to the infant classrooms.

The student teacher is almost in tears. 'Amy was sitting right there,' she points to the desk where I had sat yesterday. 'I went into the corridor to get her coat and when I came back she was gone. She's not in the toilets. She's not in the playground.' Her voice trembles and she covers her face with her hands.

'Go and tell the Head,' says Ms Talmur briskly. 'I'll get my car and drive along the road out of town and Professor Miller can drive the other way.'

She turns to me. 'Solomon. Would you have any idea in which direction a young child might wander off?'

'I'll have a look about.'

Why am I the one who knows where to go? I walk through the playground and across the football field at the back. Through the long grass and into the wood. I can see the cemetery ahead of me, the tombstones outlined against the sky. I begin to run.

As I climb up onto the broken dyke I see her coming through the gate at the other end. It has taken her longer. She has come by the road and her legs are shorter, but she is hurrying. Trotting very quickly up the main path to the back.

There is a vile stink in the air, rising from the ground below me. I look down. There is a huge sheet of green tarpaulin covering the fallen tree and the wide crater of the root hole. Rainwater has collected in puddles lying on the dips of the sheeting. Small stagnant pools with scum gathering on their surface.

She is directly beneath me and would have fallen right in had I not shouted.

'Amy,' I call loudly.

She smiles and looks up at once. Almost as though she had expected someone to be there. Waiting for her.

'Solomon?'

Not me anyway. I could tell by her voice and the expression on her upturned face.

'Your dad's worried about you.' I jump down, avoiding the tarpaulin-covered hole.

'Daddy?' She looks about her as if expecting to see him. I take her hand. She drags on my arm, and glances over her shoulder as I lead her away.

Her father is getting out of his car as we reach the entrance. 'You shouldn't have come down here to see me,' he says severely. 'I told you to wait in the school and I would collect you.'

He picks her up and hugs her close. The little face crumples up.

'But . . . you called on me to come. Hurry up, you said . . . or . . .' she glances about vaguely. 'Somebody . . . called me . . .'

'Silly girl,' he says, and kisses her. 'You've imagined that.'

Ms Talmur drew up in her car, and in the fuss and conversation no one was paying any attention to what Amy was saying.

Except me.

'Promise you will always wait for me at the school,' Professor Miller says to her.

'Don't worry,' Ms Talmur pats Amy's soft curls. 'I won't let her out of my sight.'

For a moment it was as if I saw them both through the wrong end of a telescope. Something briefly echoes in my head, and I turn without realising it to look at the far end of the graveyard.

'Does this place interest you, Solomon?' Professor Miller follows my gaze.

'What? Oh, yes.'

'It's very old,' he goes on, 'one of the most fascinating places I have ever worked in.'

'I like the stones, the colours. And the markings . . .' I hesitate. 'They tell you things.'

'Don't they just?' he agrees at once. 'Every single one is an individual tribute to the art of the stonemason. Each humble tradesman or worker would have his own emblem to show his craft.' He laughs. 'Even a miller had one.' He walks across to a very old stone. 'Look, this one has a sheaf of corn and the weighing scales. Not that millers were very popular. It was a widely held belief that they were dishonest, taking more than was their due of the corn they ground.'

He moves along the path to show me another stone. 'This person must have belonged to the hammermen. They had the right to use the royal crown as their symbol, though there were lots of different trades which used a hammer.' He rubs some dust from the stone. 'That looks like an anvil just below, so it was probably a blacksmith.'

He stops at the end of the path. 'The whole place is alive with history . . . apart from this bit.'

We have walked the full length of the main avenue to the back wall with the wood beyond.

He points to the ground. At the fallen rowan tree. 'That was the only thing that grew here and we had to take it out. Now look at it. It has rotted so very quickly that it had to be covered up. We think there are bad drains down below there. The air all around is quite foul.' He pulls aside the edge of the sheeting.

Ms Talmur gags suddenly and gropes in her pocket for her hankie. She turns her head away and I gaze in horror at the swarming mass of dank vegetation at our feet. The soil is a moving mound of brown and green slime. It is crawling with maggots.

'Merciful heaven!' Professor Miller drops the sheeting. 'I do apologise. I had no idea it had reached that state.' He ushers us away.

He doesn't seem to have noticed that the poison has spread. Now that the tree is down everything around it is dying. Decay is creeping out from its base in an ever-widening circle. The grass edges of the nearby avenues are turning brown. Further down the wall the tiny spring flowers wedged in the rocks have lost their blooms.

'Strange to have a tree like that,' I say as we walk back to the gate, 'just the one planted there.'

'Not really,' says Ms Talmur. 'It's an old custom in this country, to plant a single rowan. There's one growing by the door of practically every croft house in Scotland. They are supposed to deter evil spirits.'

And now it's gone.

She laughs, a shrill cawing, like the rooks in the tall trees of the wood. 'Call me superstitious if you like. I've already told Solomon that I'm the seventh child of a seventh child, and perhaps that makes me more sensitive to atmosphere. I don't know. But I tell you this,' she wraps her coat more tightly around her, 'I don't like this place, Professor Miller. It may be fascinating to you, but I don't like your graveyard at all.'

We go through the gate at the end.

'I don't know how Amy got in.' Professor Miller stops to re-lock the padlock. 'I mustn't have secured this properly.'

I watch him do it. He doesn't seem the type of person who would be careless enough to leave without fastening the padlock. Then I remember something. Last night the teenagers had said the gate was padlocked, yet when I came from Peter's house it was lying open. Who or what wants the gate left unlocked and why?

'Don't you have any workmen here today?' Ms Talmur asks as they move towards the cars.

'No, and perhaps not for some time. There may be a

63

problem.' Professor Miller pauses for a moment or two. 'Oh, I might as well tell you. It will be in the local newspaper this week anyway. It's almost certain that smallpox victims were interred here. I will have to do a search of the Burial Register in Glasgow before we commence exhumations.'

Ms Talmur shivered. 'The disease can't still be active, surely?'

'Probably not. There were bodies of over a hundred years old removed from a graveyard at Christchurch in Spitalfields in London fairly recently. When the virus was taken from the smallpox scabs it was found to be non-viable. However, one can't take risks where public health is concerned. So, we will have to make the area more secure before we can begin opening the graves and moving the cadavers. Perhaps erect a fence and employ security guards. It appears that youths hang around here after dark.'

No more they don't.

'I thought there was a night watchman,' I say casually.

'There was . . .' he hesitates. 'Silly superstitions. He packed in the other night. Said he heard noises, saw things. Out of a bottle probably. Then his dog ran off. A big mangy brute of an animal. He said he wasn't staying without it.'

Before she climbs into her dad's car, Amy runs over. Ms Talmur bends and kisses the top of her head. But it is to me that the child comes, flinging her arms around my waist and hugging me close. The two adults watch, smiling. They don't hear what she whispers.

'Thank you, Solomon, for saving me.' Her little face is peaked and anxious.

'I'll drive you home, Solomon,' says Ms Talmur.

Before I can say a word she has take my rucksack and put it in her car.

'We'll call at the school first and tell the staff that Amy is quite safe,' she says. 'I can't imagine why she wandered off like that.' She stops before she turns the key in the ignition. 'Can you?'

I stare straight ahead out of the car window. It is raining again. I take a deep breath.

'There is something wrong in that place,' I say.

'Yes,' she says slowly. 'Yes, I do agree.' Still she does not start the car. Her fingers clench the rim of the steering wheel. 'And it's more than just our imagination, isn't it, Solomon?'

Chapter 15

'Thanks for the lift.' I'm out of the car fast, but she is faster. She is up the path and at the front door beside me.

'I want a word with your dad.'

'He's out just now.'

'I'll wait.' She follows me into the house. The living-room door is open and he is slumped in front of the telly.

'Mr Morris.' She goes right in and stands in front of him. He leaps up, stuffing his shirt into his trousers. He is grey and tired, but he's had a shave. Or rather, tried to. Small cuts fleck his skin, his face pitted with the permanent roadworks of life.

'Ms Talmur,' she holds out her hand. 'I'm a teacher at the school. We met earlier. Remember? I collected your son this morning. I would like to talk to you about his school work.'

'Of course, of course,' he says. Instant charm on his tongue like clotted cream. 'Solomon's told me all about you.'

Bad move, Dad, this one's very sharp.

'I doubt it,' she says crisply. 'I only met him yesterday.'

He barely breaks his stride. 'Nevertheless,' he says, 'I'm sure a lot came of it.' He shakes her hand enthusiastically. 'Sol, put the kettle on, would you?'

He turns to her. 'Any time you want to talk, I'm here.' He lowers his voice. 'His work might not be so good at the moment. Been a bit difficult for both of us over the last months. We're having to cope on our own now.'

'Many people do, Mr Morris.' She goes on quickly, 'And I'd rather Solomon remained in the room. This is about his life and he must be told what is happening.'

My dad's eyes narrow. He has a close, foxy look on his face.

'And what, exactly, is happening?'

'Solomon, your son –' she turns to me. 'Solomon,' she says my name quietly 'has severe learning difficulties. In fact,' she raises her voice, 'he can scarcely read or write.'

My dad smiles. A great big open welcoming grin. 'You're new. Aren't you? We've been through all this lots of times with the school. It will work out in good time. Children mature at different rates. He'll catch up soon enough.'

'No, he won't,' she says. 'And I can hardly believe that no one has told you this before. He won't.' She stares up at him until he is forced to meet her gaze. 'HE WILL NOT CATCH UP. He will never acquire basic reading skills. Not without special help and a lot of extra work.'

There is a great silence in the room.

Then my dad laughs. An infectious happy sound, full of merriment and promise. 'You're a good girl,' he says. 'So dedicated and concerned, but you musn't worry so much. We'll get there in the end.' He slips his arm around her shoulder. 'Come and have some tea.'

But this is no Hamelin child following the Pied Piper. She slides away from him at once and turns again to face him.

'Will you listen?' she asks him. Then she turns to me. 'Or will you?' She speaks to me directly. 'Solomon, you have a problem. You cannot deal with it until you recognise that you have it. I can help you, but only if you accept that you need help.'

The truth lies like a stone between us.

'Leave the boy alone.' Dad comes over and stands beside me. 'We'll manage fine by ourselves. We always have.' There is a touch of desperate bravado in his voice. 'Eh, Sol?' And he punches me gently on the arm.

I'm watching her face. She's looking at my dad. His charm has slid right off her and lies like soiled silk at her feet. And suddenly I see him with her eyes. A big bumbling man in a drab room, bluffing his way through life.

She set her face and then speaks clearly and distinctly. 'Mr

Morris, I notice that in this, your living room, there are no magazines or books. I find that . . . unusual.' She glances around. 'Not even a newspaper.' She stares hard at him. 'I want you to think about what I have said. I am asking Solomon to come to me for tutoring. It may be too late for you. Solomon's life is just beginning.'

His face is open with shock. As he struggles to reply, she leaves. He goes into the kitchen. I follow him. He tears open a soup packet. Empties it into a pan. Adds water. Little dustings of powder spill on the worktop, the cooker, his shaking hands.

'Got the chance of some work tomorrow,' he says, beating nervously with a spoon at the lumpy mixture. 'Might be a good few weeks in it too. Weather's picking up. I love being outside when the nights get shorter, and the evenings stretch out, long and warm. It's so beautiful, the smell of spring flowers, the promise of summer.'

I blink. I can't focus. It's a stranger who stands in the kitchen, who walks between the cooker and the table putting soup into bowls and buttering bread. He clatters the dishes noisily.

'Reminds me of a time I was on one of the islands. Eriskay, I think it was. We were laying the new gas pipe line, and what a laugh we had one night. Talk about a joke. I'll tell you a good one. This particular night, you see, we had just started to unload the –'

'You can't read.'

He slurps his soup, breaks off a bit of bread and stuffs it in his mouth. 'Don't be daft.'

It's all so clear now. Why he never helped me with the letters or the words. He didn't know how to.

'You can't read.'

'Course I can.' He picks up the soup packet. 'Chicken and leek soup. Another winner from our country kitchen. To prepare three brimming bowlfuls, simply add one litre of water, bring to the boil and simmer gently for five minutes.'

68

He tosses it on to the table. 'Satisfied?'

Set a thief to catch a thief, takes one to know one.

All his life he's been doing what I do with reading. Only, he's been doing it longer, so he's much better at it.

I sit back in my chair and fold my arms. I keep my eyes on his face. 'Ingredients,' I recite. 'Water. Cornflour. Leek. Chicken. Flavourings. Salt. Hydrogenated Vegetable Oil. Flavour Enhancers. If this product disappoints in any way, please return the packet, stating why, where and when purchased and we will send a refund. Statutory rights unaffected.'

I lean forward and pick up the soup packet. I throw it at him. 'You can't read.'

He doesn't answer.

'The stories . . . all the stories.' My voice is breaking. 'You made them up.'

'What if I did? I – '

'You make everything up!'

'Sol, don't be like that. Don't look at me like that.'

But he's talking to an empty chair.

Chapter 16

Now.

All the colours are in my head, whirling and spinning and clashing together, my mind a broken kaleidoscope of red and green and gold.

I charge upstairs and hurtle into my room.

I tear down the posters, rip the fantasy from my ceiling and walls. Pull off silvered unicorns and pale princesses. Turreted castles fall. Elves and goblins, bright cartoon characters, things of his imagination and mine. I'm going to kill them all. I drag down brilliant-hued jungles with blue and yellow gaudy parrots. Trample them under my feet. Stand on the crumpled paper, crush and grind the tarnished dreams into my worn brown carpet.

Lies. Lies. Make-believe and fairy tales. Now the truth is here. The walls of my life, drab, torn and graffitied.

And the grey comes flooding in. Up into my nostrils, rolling through me like a sea fog. Into my life. Into my dreams. Cold and dismal, thin vapour slipping around me as I walk. And I'm looking for someone and calling their name. Some wailful thin and reedy voice answers me. Faintly mewing and carrying me forward to find its owner. But there's nothing I can do. There is a pit before me, crawling with vermin and worms. I cannot help. I cannot.

And the next day the dream is still with me. In Watkins' morning reveille its tendrils are still wrapped around my brain.

I am cold. By lunchtime I am shaking and ill.

Peter is sent with me to the medical room to sit out for an hour. My arm aches but there is no itch, and when I pull back my sleeve to look at the wound there is barely a mark on my skin.

And as I do so, she passes by. Did I know she would? The medical room is just by the staffroom door.

She tuts. Presses her cool hand on my arm. 'Nothing there now,' she says. She pulls my sleeve back down. 'I'll get you some tea.'

My heart is crashing inside my chest. Rhythms of panic cascading through me. She comes back with the tea and sits while I drink it. Peter gets up, walks to the window and looks out into the playground. Ms Talmur takes the mug from my fingers and sets it down on the floor. Puts her fingers under my chin and holds my head, searching my eyes.

'Well? Shall I speak to the Head? Get you out of class to come to me for tuition?' She lets go abruptly and my head drops down.

Then . . . I nod.

'Thank God for that,' and she's gone.

'Way to go, Sol,' says Peter softly.

So, now, I'm in the infants. If it wasn't for Amy I think I'd have chucked it right off.

'There's that boy,' chants one. 'The one who broke things and shouted. Why is he back?'

'To help me,' says Amy, at once, 'cos I'm new.' She slips her little hand into mine and I sit down beside her.

Oh, do I need courage, the courage of a lifetime. For a lifetime.

She scatters coloured beads in her counting tray, amber, amethyst, turquoise and red. They glitter and roll. Her chubby pink fingers grasp them and place them deftly in number order. I try to copy her, watching her slyly with a sidelong glance. She giggles as she sees me.

'No cheating, Solomon,' she whispers. 'It's got to be YOU that does it yourself.'

And I try.

I really do.

And does it work?

71

Maybe one time in ten.

'Better than none at all,' says this witch of a teacher that I have now, as she displaces the beads and sends them scattering in disorder across the table.

'Now try letters,' she flicks out a set of cards.

I feel my face flush. They are printed in extra large type and illustrated with babyish drawings.

She puts her hand on my shoulder. 'Please try to be patient and go along with this for the moment, Solomon. I need to find out what you can and cannot do.'

So I put the dog with the longest tail, and the one with the biggest ears and the shortest legs where they have to go. And I put the ice lolly and the igloo and the snowman together beside the word COLD and the iron and the chips and the fire with the word HOT.

'Now we'll try some letter order.' She puts down a bundle of interlocking alphabet letters and writes out the words she wants us to make.

The child beside me absorbs the information and moves on. I repeat the task six times and the seventh time I get it wrong. I seem to have no ability to remember the order in which the letters have to go. No power of recall to help me get it right each time.

I glance at Amy. She is frowning in concentration, tongue between teeth. She reaches for another card and as she does so the sleeve of her blouse slides back. There is an angry red weal on her wrist.

'What's that?' I ask her.

She touches it with the fingers of her other hand. 'It's sore,' she says.

'How did it happen?'

'I think . . . in the graveyard yesterday,' she says. 'I scraped it on the branch of the dead tree.'

My voice is dry with fear. 'Didn't your mum notice when you got washed last night?'

She thinks for a minute. 'It wasn't there last night.'

I look round for Ms Talmur. As I stand up to call her over, the school bell rings. The infants have an earlier dismissal time. She is sorting out the wee ones' bags, bundling them into their jackets. Professor Miller is at the door for Amy. I see them talking together. Then Ms Talmur beckons to me.

'Professor Miller will be working in the central archives office in Glasgow for an hour or two. He wants to know if you and I would be interested in going there after school today. They have uncovered some material relating to the burial ground and the history of this area. He thought we might like to have a look at it.'

I help her clear up the classroom. The blobs of modelling clay, the bits of paper. This time next year these kids will have learnt their letters, know so many words, move forward to the next class.

'Where will I be?

'Right.' She puts her coat on. 'Let's go. We'd better stop off and let your dad know where you'll be.'

'He's out,' I say.

She raises an eyebrow.

'Honestly, he is. He got some work, and left a message with a neighbour to say he'd be very late and I'd not to wait up.'

God! I must have been daft not to notice. All those times, instead of writing me a note he'd leave word with someone to tell me. 'Your dad was in too much of a rush today,' Mrs Gilmore would call across the garden as I left for school. 'Said to tell you.' Then she'd trot out whatever message he'd given her.

Now I remember. His birthday cards. He drew pictures on them. A big X and then lots of cartoons of him and me. I used to show them round the class. Dead proud. Thought they were special. Didn't realise it was because he couldn't write a message.

Once, after Mum had left, when I came downstairs the milk boy was in the kitchen. Dad was making him a cup of tea while he filled in some form for him.

'Scalded myself,' he waved a bandaged hand under my nose. 'Devlin's very kindly being my secretary this morning. Have a bacon butty, lad. Need to give you an extra big tip at Christmastime.'

And the boy went away happily chewing his sandwich, both of us fooled.

Chapter 17

More shades of grey. Buildings and people. Tints and hues of absence of colour. Smirring rain glossing the pavements with an oily sheen.

A name, suddenly, on the wall of a street flashing past. Golden Road. I close my eyes to shut it out. She had made me say it, over and over. Traced the letters with my fingers. 'That's where I'll be.'

She had written it down. I threw the piece of paper in the bin as soon as she left. Crushing it up in my hand first. Maybe she knew I would, and that's why she had made me repeat it to her, again and again.

'Golden Road. Get the 44 bus and ask to be put off at the traffic lights. The close is just opposite, top flat. Come any time.'

Standing in the hall with her suitcase, by the open front door. I turned my head away so that I did not see her go.

But I heard. 'Solomon, I'm sorry.'

I heard. The door closing.

And she was gone. I was left.

But I didn't care so much. She would never help me do up my tie or my shoelaces, whereas Dad would. She was the boring one who made me try to write my homework over and over. The one who forced me to sound out the spelling words, while he only glanced at my reading book and then told me the story the way it ought to be.

What a dope I am.

She loved me.

'Feeling sick?' Ms Talmur asks.

I shake my head and open my eyes. We have stopped at the

traffic lights. There is the close mouth. Just there. My eyes travel upwards. A lamp shines in the window at the top of the building. I look at it. My swollen heart, a bruised plum in my chest.

The blurred red of the traffic light throbs ready to burst. Ms Talmur stares at it, then glances at me. She frowns. Gently, softly, she stretches her fingers out towards me.

NO!

Then suddenly, her hand moves down, and she switches on the car radio. Loudly.

The music fills the empty space.

The light changes and she accelerates off on the amber. She turns the wheel and we cross the intersection. Carefully I exhale my breath. I touch my face. It is wet.

'Watch out for a brick building on the left,' she says. 'Two stories high, with pillars at the front.'

She is driving more slowly. Peoples' faces are closer, expressions more detailed. Experience the master mason who has carved on these blank stones. Lines of anxiety, grooves of grief and pain, channels of laughter and love.

I see it first. 'There.' I point.

She gives me a quick smile. 'Well done.'

I shrug and look away.

Look away. Look away. Beulah. I wish I was in Dixie, oh yeah.

She draws in and parks by the roadside.

My legs are weighted heavy as I get out of the car. Like walking through water in the swimming pool, trying to hurry, pushing forward, wading in syrup.

Useless.

Like me.

No point in trying.

What for?

My skin is hot and my hands shake. I stick them in my pocket and hunch up my shoulders. Then she has locked the car and is round to my side. She tucks her arm through mine,

76

and walks smartly beside me.

'Cheer up, Solomon. Please,' she says. 'I know your head must be aching. You've done a tremendous amount of work today, and you probably feel that you've not got very far.' She laughs. 'And to be quite truthful, you haven't. But the beginning is going to be the worst. You haven't tried to learn anything for such a long time that it is going to be tough for you to start with.'

I stop in the courtyard and face her. 'It's going to be tough most of the time. Isn't it?'

She stares straight back. 'Yes,' she says. 'Want to give up right now?'

I shuffle my feet. 'Maybe.'

'OK,' she says lightly. 'Back to Warrior Watkins tomorrow then.' She draws her arm away and walks on without me.

'I just said, "Maybe",' I call after her.

She swings round and wags her finger in my face. 'Well don't,' she snaps. 'I don't deal with "maybes" or "perhaps" or "nearly" people. I'm not going to waste my time with the "almosts". She grabs my arm again. 'Solomon, you couldn't be a "maybe" even if you tried. Come on, let's see what Professor Miller has found out.'

We go into the building and ask for him. They buzz his office and direct us up. It's on the top floor. As the lift doors open he comes to meet us from his room. He is very excited.

'I think I may have found something that might interest you,' he says. 'In fact, several things. Some to do with the smallpox victims. They died in an epidemic during the 1850s. They were all children, many of them brothers and sisters. Tragic really. But there is also some material relating back to the seventeenth and eighteenth century. There was a witch hunt in this area. The last person to be burned as a witch in Scotland was in Dornoch, in the Highlands, in 1722. However, there was a trial here the previous year. I've put the relevant documents aside for us to look at.'

I see beyond him into the office. There is a figure standing there. The bars of an electric fire glow bright red behind it, giving it a hard black outline. It reaches out its finger and points at me.

'No!' I step back.

Ms Talmur turns to me. 'What is it, Solomon? What's wrong?'

The professor looks round. 'It's only Amy,' he says. 'She begged to be allowed to come, especially when she heard that Solomon was going to be here. I promised her mother that I wouldn't keep her too late.'

The child moves forward into the light, and now I know her. All senses are stripped, my eyes see all there is to see, my ears hear every whisper.

I recognise her as she comes towards me.

Professor Miller's daughter.

Chapter 18

'Solomon,' Amy pulls on my hands. 'You're cold. Come to the fire.'

She has been sitting on the rug in the office colouring in picture outlines. 'Do you like these?' She shows me her drawings.

I nod my head. I crouch down beside her. My eyes are suddenly full of tears and I don't know why. She chatters on and I take a few gulps of air.

'Look at this, Solomon,' Ms Talmur calls to me. 'It is the Burial Record Book.' She reads from the cover, '"Register of Burials of Stone Mill Graveyard." It even has a proper name, your graveyard. There must have been a mill around there at some time. I suppose being close to the river it was a natural place to build one.'

I get up and walk to the table. The professor shows us the old history books of the area, copies of letters and the Sheriff's deposition to have the graveyard closed.

'The Environmental Health Department have consulted with the Health and Safety Executive,' says Professor Miller. 'We're going to have to work on the assumption that there could be a risk from infection. The soil is very wet, in fact there is probably an underground stream running there, but that is actually to our benefit. The smallpox scabs would have to have been kept very dry for any infection to survive.'

'So, what will happen now?' asks Ms Talmur.

'The officials will agree a code of practice for general conditions, and also for safe operations, such as digging and removal of suspect remains. They have to make sure that protective clothing, safety boots, respirators, etc. are being used. They will make filter canisters and a special type of disinfectant available. First of all, though, they are going to make the site secure. In fact they're doing that just now. We can have a look at it later on our way home.'

The professor picks up one of the books and a file from the table. 'I thought this might be of more interest to you. It's a much older historical reference, and concerns an incident which took place in this town hundreds of years ago. It's a collection of letters and trial notes edited and printed by the local minister of the day.'

Ms Talmur opens the file and picks out a yellowed sheet of paper. She squints at it. 'A trial?' she queries. 'What for?'

'Witchcraft. Sixteenth- and seventeenth-century Scotland was famous for witch-hunting. It became common in every part of this country. It started off with minor punishments for those unfortunate enough to be convicted but quite soon almost everyone found guilty was burned to death.'

Ms Talmur peers closely at the script in front of her. 'Gosh, Solomon. You think you've got problems. Seventeenth-century Scots spelling is almost impossible to read. Take a look at this.' She holds it out.

MALEFICE.

The word uncurls out from the page and spits at me.

'What . . . what is that word?'

Professor Miller leans over my shoulder. 'It is a Scottish word for witchcraft, or the practice of evil.'

There is a deep dark shadow in the room.

Stretching out over the earth.

A lengthening darkness unfolding, slowly chilling the air.

An evil purpose spreading its deadly intent.

Now . . . I can see from the window, down into the street. Onto the stupid and puny humans scuttling about below me.

My breath hisses through my teeth. Through narrowed eyes I watch them. They have tried to grind me down, now I will crush them.

'Solomon,' she speaks my name.

'Miss?'

She looks at me keenly. 'Are you quite well?'

Oh, yes, very well and getting better. Growing stronger all the time.

She is standing close by the window. In her smart suit, small feet in high heels. Her pretty face is right against the glass pane.

Now.

One hard push and it would shatter. Splintering crystal pieces out and down like a cascading waterfall. Great shards of glass slicing through flesh . . .

'Solomon!' she says sharply.

'Miss?'

'Sit down.' She pushes me gently into a chair. 'Have you eaten anything today?'

I shake my head.

'We'll go to McDonalds on the way home,' she says.

Home. I want to go home. My hands are trembling. Amy comes over and puts her hands in mine. They are warm. She smiles at me.

'You're all right, aren't you?' she says. 'It wasn't good, what happened long ago.'

'No,' says Ms Talmur, 'it wasn't good.'

'Ignorance and fear can poison people's minds,' said Professor Miller. 'That's why these poor women were condemned to die. People like to blame their ill luck on someone else. They were used as scapegoats for a bad harvest, cattle disease or inclement weather.'

'Or trying to cure a sickly child, and be blamed when she dies.' The thought is in my mind, and I say the words.

'Yes, indeed,' says the professor, 'that was often the case. Sometimes they were healers or "spey-wifes"', and as they didn't have modern medicine to aid them, their patients frequently did not recover.'

'It's a fascinating subject,' says Ms Talmur. 'Would you

mind if I borrowed these books and letters for a few days?'

'No,' says the professor.

'NO!' I cry out.

They look up in surprise.

'It's horrible. What they did . . . at the trial and after . . .'

She takes the books, letters, papers and places them carefully in a document case. 'I'll take these home and read them through.' She snaps the lock closed. She notices me still watching her. 'Don't worry, Solomon. I'm not very squeamish.'

I shake my head. 'It's not that. It's just . . . when you're reading it . . . be careful.'

She puts her head on one side and looks at me. 'Why?'

I cannot answer. I do not know why.

'You think it might disturb me? I'm not of a nervous disposition. But if it will make you feel better I won't do it tonight. I'll wait until tomorrow morning.' She smiles at me. 'Now come on, let's go and have something to eat.'

I follow them downstairs and across the courtyard. Professor Miller, Amy, and my teacher. They walk ahead of me chatting casually. They do not know. They cannot feel it. But it's there. Thicker than air, unseen and deadly, seeping like nuclear fallout or a vague drifting gas, around and into every orifice. Licking at the dark corners of your mind, searching out the flaws, the imperfections. Spreading doubt and mistrust. Feeding on fear, becoming ever more powerful.

Awakening evil.

I watch them.

And I'm afraid.

Chapter 19

They're erecting a huge fence around the graveyard when we stop on our way home. About two metres high and with murderous barbed wire coiled along the top. All the way around the perimeter. Well clear of the dyke.

I walk quickly through to the back wall as the professor and Ms Talmur speak to each other.

The tree is unrecognisable. A heap of decay and withered death surround it. Nothing appears to have been moved. I lift the end of the tarpaulin with the toe of my boot. The stink is unbearable.

'There must be a lot of stagnant water lying down there.' One of the workmen who are hammering the sheetboard together has dropped the nail gun on the damp earth.

'Never smelled the likes of that before,' says the other.

'Bet there's rats,' says the first. 'Glad it's not me doing that job.'

He picks up his tools and they move on rapidly.

I cast around me. What am I seeking here? I don't know. I return to the main gate. Amy has not got out of her dad's car. White face pressed against the window.

There is someone talking to Professor Miller.

'Most of the extra equipment has been delivered now. Heavy duty polythene bags, safety boots and helmets, and the respirators.'

I recognise Mr Frame.

'I'll have to draft in more men though. That's the second worker that's just up and left without giving notice. Gerry Nisbet and Joe Service, both within days of each other. One of their wives, Alison Service, has been at my office every morning. More interested in his pay than his whereabouts right enough. Seems he goes on drinking sprees from time to time.'

They continue their discussion. I touch Ms Talmur's sleeve. 'Will you look at Amy's wrist? She has a cut like the one I had. Says she caught it on the rowan tree that was taken down. Says it's sore.'

Amy pulls back her sleeve. There is only a faint red line marking her skin. Ms Talmur examines it.

'I think it's OK. It hasn't broken the surface.' She shows it to Professor Miller.

'I don't think it's gone septic. Just a scratch, really.' He buttons her blouse cuff. He smiles at me. 'It's this place, Solomon, isn't it? Making you restless. Everything has remained quiet for so long that all this disturbance is worrying.' He puts his hand on my shoulder. 'We'll have it all moved and cleared in a few weeks and then they'll build the bridge and divert the river and it will be finished.'

Not finished. No. Beginning.

'Actually, graveyards weren't always dull places,' he went on. 'In the Middle Ages it was quite common practice to hold the town market in the kirkyard. Lots of places still have their medieval market cross in the parish graveyard. It dates back to before the Reformation, when folk would come to monasteries and churches from all over Scotland to celebrate the major religious festivals. Naturally they needed to buy food and drink, and that soon expanded into general trading, cattle dealing and a place for farm labourers to arrange which farm they would work on for the next year. They were known as the "Hiring Fairs".'

'You mean thay had cattle and sheep wandering among the graves?' Ms Talmur asks, looking about her. 'I can hardly believe it.'

'Oh, yes.' Professor Miller laughs. 'They used the table stones as counters and the walls of mausoleums like a blackboard to mark the prices of their goods. It's hard for us to imagine it. Nowadays our graveyards are such quiet and reverent places. But in earlier times the markets became quite jolly occasions.

'In fact people were having so much fun, and often on a Sunday too, that the authorities decided to put a stop to it. The fairs were so well established however, especially in small rural places, that mostly the new laws were ignored. It took a long time before they moved off to a different place in the town.'

'I'm sure it didn't happen here,' I say.

No, I think you're right, Solomon. This is a different type of place altogether. The surveyors think that the river must have originally flowed in this direction a long time ago. They have done test drillings. There is a water table right beneath us, which is probably why the ground is so wet underneath. They can also tell by the vegetation and the soil make-up. So when we redirect the water it will be a case of putting things back as they were.'

He puts Amy in the car and takes me and Ms Talmur to the edge of the road where the river runs down from behind the wood past the graveyard, and shows us where it is being dammed. There is a piece of plant machinery at work dredging at the river edge.

'So far they have come up with six supermarket trolleys, a couple of old mattresses and about twenty dozen empty beer cans.'

The long arm is spooning out big chunks of mud. Cold, dark-brown liquid pours from the metal shovel as it lifts high into the air. The scoop up-ends and, with a great sucking squelch, deposits its load. Then it swings back to clutch greedily down again into the depths of the river.

We turn away.

There is a sudden shout from the dredger operator. Ms Talmur's gaze is directed at something beyond my shoulder. She puts her hand to her mouth, her face turning pale with shock.

'Dear God!' Professor Miller grips her firmly and steers her towards the car.

I swivel round. I cannot move.

There is a body straddled across the prongs of the metal dredging scoop. Fronds of algae cling to the face and arms as the river water pours from this man's clothing. He is spread crossways with one arm caught in the metal teeth and dangling down. Limp and crushed, he is definitely dead. He is wearing workman's brown overalls.

Again a dream.

Fire burning. Crackling. Vicious and hungry. And smoke. Billowing, thick and foggy. I cannot breathe.

The whispering in my ear and the powerful urge to get up, go now, now, to the graveyard. I've fallen asleep lying on top of my bed. The cheeseburger that Ms Talmur forced me to eat earlier lies thick and undigested in my stomach. Her own teeth were chattering and fingers trembling as she drank her tea in the café.

'There is a very real sense of unease in that place,' she said. 'I'll be glad when they've moved . . . everything . . . and the river covers it up.'

It's too late, I think. Whatever it is, was, has now been released, is out, gaining strength and seeking more.

And now I have to get there. I'm needed.

'Ssssolomon.' A whisper beside my face. 'Come to me.'

Like a sleepwalker I open my bedroom door. My father is on the landing walking towards me on stockinged feet.

'Sorry, son.' He points to his shoes in his hand. 'I tried not to wake you as I came in.' He peers into my face. 'You OK?'

I pass my hand across my face. 'Where am I?'

'Here,' my dad takes my arm, 'you're only half awake.' He guides me into my room and pulls the quilt back. 'Lie down now.' He sits on the bed. 'I could always tell you a story,' he says sadly, 'to get you back to sleep.' He gives me a faint smile. 'I guess not, though.'

He tucks the cover round me and waits until he thinks I'm sleeping before going away.

I take the ring from under my pillow. The ring I had found in the graveyard. It seems to burn my hand as I twist it round and round in my fingers. It's cold and greasy in my grasp.

The lettering on the inside. Two words engraved into the gold. A curtain draws back. I know what they are, who they are. I heard those names spoken aloud this afternoon by Mr Frame.

Joe Service – disappeared. His wife looking for him – Alison Service. The letter I couldn't read. The beginning of my own name. The one I draw upside down and back to front. The S. It was in the middle of her name, and blocked me from understanding what was written on the ring. "Alison & Joe – FOREVER".

It must have been his wedding ring.

I know this.

She can search for him from now until hereafter. From where he has gone there is no return.

Chapter 20

Amy is sick. Early, next day, before the morning break, I saw her little face flushed, her hands shake as she holds her pencil.

'You OK?'

Her eyes glittered as she raised her lids to answer me. The lip trembled. I stood up and fetched some water from the sink.

'Here.' I thrust a cup under her chin. I have to hold it as she drinks. I look around me. Ms Talmur is busy. I wring out Amy's hankie and dab awkwardly at her forehead.

'Oh, dear, Amy. You don't seem very well today.' Ms Talmur has noticed at last. 'Solomon, will you take her to the medical room? I'll call her home and ask for someone to collect her.'

I sit with Amy until her mother arrives.

'My arm's sore again,' she says quietly to me, leaning her head against my shoulder.

I look down at the soft curls. 'Let me see.' The skin is red, and the darker blotchy patches are hot and itchy.

'Nettles,' I say firmly. 'Jaggy nettles. You've rubbed up against them and didn't notice.'

'Is it?' There is a great relief in her voice.

'Yeah. Definitely. Got a rash same as that dozens of times when I was your age. Needs a docken leaf. You rub it on and it takes the sting away.' I hesitate. 'I'll get you one if you like.'

She puts her hand in mine. 'I like you, Solomon,' she says. It's the first time I remember anyone ever saying that to me.

Her mum arrives and takes her away. Amy looks behind

her as she goes out the front door. A small scared glance back to me.

Without her beside me at the desk, I feel them all staring at me. Everything goes wrong. Nothing from yesterday's lesson has stayed in my head. My fingers can't manipulate the cards and number blocks. Warrior Watkins is right. I am a baboon, a clumsy ape. Even the way I hold my pencil is different, the way I write is strange. I form my numbers from the bottom upwards. No one else does that. I've watched to see.

Why can't I make my thoughts sit as words upon the paper? I can only use the words which I'm confident I can spell properly. I have to write "nice" when I mean beautiful, "good" when I'm thinking perfection. All my images and ideas are crushed and stillborn. Rainbows arc inside me, then abort, earthbound, into monochrome dullness.

'Hell, blast it!'

The sharp crack of splintered wood sounds, and despite the special triangular rubber grip which Ms Talmur has put on it, my pencil is in two pieces in my hand. I grab the jagged end and score the varnished desk top. Vicious lines of rage and frustration pouring out of me to be scraped onto the clean smooth surface. Down from my mind through my fingers to gouge a mark on the world.

Ms Talmur leans across my shoulder and plucks the pencil stump neatly from my fist.

'Solomon, there is something in particular I would like you to do for me this afternoon.'

I thrust my legs out into the passageway and slump down in my seat. She snaps her fingers in front of my eyes. I raise my head.

'Amy has gone home without her schoolbag.' She holds my gaze until I slowly start to refocus. 'I shall let you away earlier. Perhaps you could take it to her house. I shall put in some books which she might like to look at, and some drawings to colour. That should amuse her while she is in bed.'

She talks on, piling the books before me, asking me to select one or two. Her words flow over and around me. She hands me the cards to put in the bag. Bearing me up, pulling me back.

'Good,' she says finally. 'That's us organised, I think.' She hands me Amy's schoolbag. 'Off you go. Tell her all her class mates are thinking of her.' She pats my back and gives me a tiny push out the door and into the corridor.

And coming towards me, is my class. Marching along from the television room.

Melly sees me first, and gives a big smile, then shrinks back as Watkins spots her and me at the same time.

'Aha! What have we here? Our missing friend,' he shouts.

My insides grip, and a fierce pain cuts through my head.

'Enjoying the infants, are you, Solly?' He waits a second, blocking my path. 'Are you?' he repeats louder.

'Sir . . .'

I can't speak. My words slurred, my tongue caught inside my mouth.

'Sir . . .'

'He probably is, actually,' says a voice behind him.

Peter has come to the front of the line. I stare at him. He gives me a crazy grin and then turns to Watkins.

'Getting taught all the stuff he's missed. I mean, Sir. That's good isn't it?' he asks innocently.

Watkins looks him over.

'Isn't it?' Peter says again distinctly.

Watkins' eyes drop. He marshals his group. 'Come along,' he orders sharply, and the class move off.

'Stay with it, Sol,' Peter says quietly to me as he walks away.

I lean against the wall for a minute. Slowly, my mind comes unstuck and I can think again. I straighten up and walk out of the school.

And I'm thinking.

Stay with it.

Stay with it.

And I will.

For as long as I can.

When I get to her house Amy is sitting up in bed with a tight bright little smile fixed to her face.

'Not too long a visit,' says her mum going out the door. 'She's just woken up, but she's still very tired.'

I dump the bag on the bed cover. Then I look at her more closely. 'What's the matter?'

'I had the dream again.' Her voice is quiet with fear..

'What dream?'

'The lady singing, and telling me to come to her.'

My heart thuds. 'Come where?' I ask.

'I don't know.' She shakes her head. 'I don't know.'

'What does the lady look like?'

'Sometimes like Mummy. She sounds like Mummy, or maybe Daddy, or somebody else I know. She whispers in my head.'

Now I am truly alarmed. 'Did you tell your mum or dad about it?'

She nods. 'They say it's a bad dream and it will go away. Will it go away, Solomon?'

'Sure it will.' I sit on the bed and take out the docken leaves I have picked as I walked from the school. I start to rub her arm with them. As they shred under my fingers I can feel her muscles coiled tight, her body tense.

'Listen.' I grope about desperately for something, anything to take her concentration away from her fear. 'Listen,' I say, 'I'll tell you a story . . .'

Chapter 21

He was standing by the gate as I came down our street.
Chatting away to one of the neighbours, arms waving about,
roaring with laughter. Some great tale being told.

He saw me coming then, and his face beamed with
happiness. 'Have to go now, Sol's dinner to fix,' he broke off
his story, and I could see she was disappointed. 'I'll tell you
the rest another time.' He gave her a wink as he picked up his
bags of shopping.

'You got some work today.' I nodded at the groceries.

'Yeah, a bit of casual out of town, no social snoopers, and a
sub until next Friday.' He lugged the bags into the kitchen.
'You go and watch the telly, I'll do that,' he says quickly as I
go to help.

I am already lifting the first carrier to place it on the
worktop. The chink of bottles sounds as I put it down.

Silence.

'Look, Sol . . .' he starts as I open up the bag.

I take the drink out and place it on the counter. 'Don't say
a word.' I can feel my throat thick with tears. 'I've listened to
you all my life. Who do you listen to? This?' I point to the
bottle.

He laughs out loud. Harsh and brittle. 'Don't be daft. It's
not a problem. Sure, I take a drop too much once in a while.
Who doesn't? Anyway, I deserve a treat tonight. I've worked
hard today.'

It's hopeless. He can't see it. He really can't. I look at him.
His eyes slide away from mine, a veiled shifting of focus.
Then they snap back at me, and I wait for what is coming.
Aggression? Charm? Excuses? Flattery?

'Sol, son,' he says quietly.

It's to be sincerity this time.

Our eyes meet.

The truth crashes into my head. An awful, terrible truth.

He can see it. He *does* know. That hesitation, the way his eyes avoided mine. He knows himself.

I give him the look that Ms Talmur gave me just before I took the flaky in her classroom and shake my head.

'You're not fooling me any more,' I say. 'I'm not staying around to watch this time. You'd better decide. It's that stuff or me.'

And now I know why my mother left. At some time she must have given him the same choice. And he had chosen the booze.

He picks up a bottle. My eyes follow his hand. His fingers unscrew the lid. He opens a cupboard and takes down a tumbler.

'You're being silly. What do you know about life? Nothing.'

My eyes are on the glass in his hand. 'Don't, Dad. Please.'

Defiance. Bravado.

He starts to tip the bottle.

I turn away.

So I'm upstairs and I'm packing my rucksack. I'm going to get as far away from here as I can. He'll be crazy drunk in an hour or two. I can't handle it this time. I am so tired. My head aches with all the exercises that Ms Talmur has made me do. The books are scattered on the floor. The coloured perspex sheet which I read through to stop the print jumping about. The dotted shapes of the letters I draw round each night. The card games she plays with me and Amy.

The pictures she drew to get me to sort out the letters, b, p and d.

I spy with my little eye.

The tall straight man with the ball at his feet.

Something beginning with . . .

b
bottle basket bed baby
d
dummy desk duckling duck
p
pencil pin pebble
b and p
baby in a pram
b and d
baby doll: baby duck.
Hours of work with the picture squares.
For what?
I knew that answer now. He had told me a few moments ago downstairs.
Nothing.
I'll chuck them in the bin. I gather a handful and then remember as I start to crush them up that a lot of this belongs to Amy. I stuff the cards and books into a plastic bag. I'll take them to her on my way to the bus station. I want to see her anyway, see if she is any better.

There is a storm on its way. The air crackles with static as I let myself softly out the front door. I'll have to hurry. I want to be clear of the town and in some bothy or lock-up before it starts. I run quickly along the lanes to the street where Amy lives.

I stop abruptly at her driveway. All the curtains are drawn back and every light in the house is on. The front door is wide open. The sound of a woman sobbing carries out into the garden. I can see into the hallway. It's Amy's mother and someone else. My teacher. They are standing together in the hallway. Ms Talmur has her arm around Amy's mother.

Outside a police car is drawn up, half on the pavement, its blue light endlessly circling.

Chapter 22

The gate was double padlocked. Everything silent. Dark and complete.

The air was close and clammy, a small breeze moved some dry fallen leaves fretfully about on the path.

'I suppose it was a crazy idea we had,' said Ms Talmur, 'to think that Amy would come back to the graveyard. It's just . . . there is something compelling about this place. She looked around her. 'There's no one here, come on,' she said.

I took my eyes from the long paths stretching out and down. I moved away from the gate towards the car.

What?

I turn back.

Nothing.

We drove to the police station. Professor Miller sat in the interview room, his head leaning back against the bare painted wall, long legs stretched out in front of him. His face is drained of colour, his lips grey. He opens his eyes briefly when we come in and nods to me.

A doctor appears and speaks to him quietly, tries to persuade the professor to take some tablets. He brushes him aside.

The duty sergeant enters with tea and cigarettes. 'There's a WPC at home with your wife, sir,' he says. 'Here, drink some of this.' He thrusts a mug under Professor Miller's face.

The professor takes it from him, looks at it stupidly, and places it carefully on the table.

'Try not to worry too much,' says the sergeant. 'Your little girl probably became feverish with that virus she had, went downstairs, got confused as to where she was, and wandered off somewhere.' He puts his hand on the professor's arm. 'She'll be tucked up in some corner. Don't fret. It's a warm night, we'll find her.'

The professor gazes at the sergeant for a moment. 'Do you really believe that?' he asks. Suddenly he springs to his feet. 'I should be out looking for her.'

The sergeant takes him by the shoulder and leads him back gently to his chair. 'Yes,' he says steadily. 'I do believe we'll find her. She's not been gone long. We've saturated the area with policemen, and these people are experts. Yes,' he says again, 'I do believe we will find her.'

The professor slumps back down in his chair, leans forward and puts his head in his hands.

It's oppressive in the small room. The professor starts to pace up and down, up and down.

A woman police officer brings more cups of inadequate tea, tries some reassuring words, leaves. The professor goes out to the toilet for a few minutes.

I stare at the wall. There is nothing to say.

Ms Talmur is tapping with her crimson nails on the edge of the table. She sees me watching.

'Sorry, Solomon,' she smiles briefly.

I shrug.

'I looked up that information,' she says brightly.

'What?'

In my head, pictures of stones and stories. The sounds of the words, rolling and crashing together. Setting off sparks to spin and twist, and flare up into the vivid colours I had created only hours earlier, making Amy laugh. She had fallen asleep, quieted. I had done that. Briefly my soul had fluttered against the tight constraining bands which held it down. And now she was threatened. In some kind of unspeakable danger, and I could do nothing.

'Yes, I read through some of the trial and background notes this morning.' Ms Talmur talking desperately. Trying to fill the silence, the misgivings, with any conversation

'It's quite an interesting tale about the woman who was burned as a witch. She lived where the kirkyard is now. No wonder there is a bad atmosphere there. They burned her within sight of the mill itself. They had diverted the river when they built the mill and it took away her water supply. She is supposed to have put a curse on the miller and all of his family.'

Himself and all of his. Forever.

'But she was a "spey-wife", well renowned for her healing powers, and he went to ask her for help when there was illness in the family.'

A miller. The symbol on the gravestone. The wheel. The water.

'What happened?' I ask.

But I know. I know what happened. Nothing I could do. Frail little thing. Too far gone for help.

'She couldn't cure the child, and everyone said it was her fault. Blamed her for the child being sick in the first place. When the little girl died they said it was a malefice.'

MALEFICE.

'She vowed at her trial she would have her revenge.'

I will.

I will have her.

The miller's daughter.

Professor Miller comes back into the room. He picks up a mug of tea, looks at it and puts it back on the table.

I needed to breathe, air. 'I'm going out for a walk,' I say.

My face and neck are damp with sweat. In the sky, great black thunder clouds are stoking up a storm. I move through the liquid air. Real and unreal. The sound of the water draws me and I go to the bridge and lean on the stone parapet. The river runs silver in the black night.

I lift my gaze from its surface. Away from the noise of the water, slap slapping on the mill-wheel paddles. The quick rush of the current in the mill-race. The creaking groan of the great oak axle slowly turning.

From here I can see the kirkyard, blue-black in the distance. A blurred outline of trees.

Stones, carved and still.

Waiting.

Waiting in the darkness.

And in that darkness something moves.

Chapter 23

I'm running. My chest is tight and sore. Breath rasping and whistling in my lungs. Branches whip against my face. Brambles tear at my legs and arms. There is a voice screaming. Out loud. The sound ripping through the trees, screaming and screaming.

It's my voice.

'Amy! Amy!'

Now I'm at the back dyke and the solid wooden fencing has been torn aside. Blasted apart as if some careless giant had passed by and trodden on it. I stare at the wood, not splintered or broken, but melted. Dissolved and warped. Curled aside to make a small space. Space enough for a child to walk through. What could do that? What power is there that would leave that mark?

I hesitate, feeling the first great lurch of fear for myself.

'Amy?' I cry out.

Beyond me the gaping dark of the cemetery.

There is a soft shudder in my head. A strange flicker which fastens on my fear. Nothing calling for me this time. No whispers in my face tonight.

Why?

Because Amy is in there. With one child captive, there is no need for two.

I hurl myself at the open space and the barbed wire comes up to meet me, scratching through my skin, dragging at my clothes to pull me back. The thick bristles are embedded in my jacket and I'm caught fast, struggling on the ground. I unzip the front of my anorak, and draw out my arms. I leave it there and crawl forwards to the foot of the dyke.

Blood on my hands and fingernails as I scramble to the top. Then I jump over and sink down knee-deep on the other side, my legs heavy with clogged and slimy liquid. I raise one foot, looking down, expecting to see thick viscous mud clinging there.

Nothing.

Then the next leg.

Nothing.

But I am sinking. The ground falling away beneath me. I am dropping down and it will close over my head and suffocate me.

I shake my feet. Must get this substance off them. I stare at them, each one. Just as that poor mad dog had done.

Then I shake my head desperately, trying to cling to my reason. Is what I see real? Or is there something there which I cannot see?

White ash blowing in the wind. Blowing and shifting. Changing, yet never moving. Remaining the same. Ash from a burning fire.

I lower my head and move my mind. Out and away.

Done it so often. In the class with Warrior Watkins. Can do it now. Switch off. Shut up. Close down.

There! Now!

I break the connection. My fear is my own and I *will* control it.

Nothing here. Nothing. The tree is gone. The tarpaulin remains.

So . . .

Down there. Underneath some broken earth and roots.

What?

A flutter again in my brain. A small fan of wind to stir up the deep-rooted fears of the unknown.

The chest was there. I knew it. Though whatever had been in it was out now. Drifting around, seeking . . . more power.

Whispers.

Someone singing. The frail, halting voice of a young child.

I pivot round, slowly. Very slowly.

Amy is sitting not so far away on the grass playing with some small stones, running them through her fingers. Clinking them together like beads.

'Amy,' I call softly.

She raises her head to me. Eyes glazed and feverish. 'Solomon,' she cries happily. 'Look what I've found.'

Now that I am closer to her I can see that they are coloured glass beads. Burning and glowing with a strange deep fire within. Blue and red and green they flash under the moonlight.

Glass beads.

No! Not glass!

Ah! I see them now! Excitement surges in me as I realise she has found the treasure! Whatever it was. It had been hidden in the box. It had taken a small child to unearth it.

And we have it! Even if the reward was only a fraction of the value, it was wealth. Money! I would be able to get away. To do what I wanted. I move forward to touch them. To hold them in my hands, dribble them down through my fingers, feel the smooth sides, touch the sharp edges.

Amy smiles a welcome. 'Want one?' She offers me a handful to choose from.

I reach out . . .

And down . . .

Then.

Amy picks up one jewel with her other hand and places it in her mouth. My hand halts, suspended in the void.

Amy stretches her hand out further to me. 'The pink one tastes nice,' she says.

A coldness creeps upon me. Along my arms, bare in my tee shirt. Through my body, into my bones.

Amy does not see diamonds and rubies as I do. It is sweets which lie in her hands, not precious jewels.

We each see what we want to see.

The workmen on that last evening in the graveyard. Joe, reaching out for gold. Gerry had sought to find his friend. And Amy, drawn in the same way any child would be tempted. By sweets.

Now I could see them too. I must have been mistaken. They *were* sweets. In her hands, on her lap, strewn beside her on the ground. Different little boxes with shiny paper. There is the smell of chocolate, the taste of aniseed and liquorice on my tongue.

I should have some too.

I hunker down in front of her and carefully, with my hand underneath hers, I flick them away, across the grass.

'See?' I say lightly, heart crashing inside my chest, 'Pretty pebbles. That's all.'

We both watch the stones fall and scatter.

There is a deep hiss of anger in my head. I shut it out.

'Come on,' I say, taking her hand. 'Your mum's waiting for you.'

She looks around her, reluctant to leave.

'She's here, my mum's here,' she says, getting up slowly. Too slowly.

'No, Amy,' I reply firmly. 'She's not. She's at home. And that's where we're going now.'

She's almost on her feet. 'But I want to stay. To hear the end of the song. Please, Solomon?'

'What song?' I hold out my arms to her.

The lady's singing it again. Just like mummy does. Can't you hear it?'

Yes. No. NO!

'No,' I say. 'I don't hear anything.'

'But she's there. Can't you see her?' says Amy.

'Where?' I ask.

She smiles at me and whispers, very softly.

'Behind you.'

Chapter 24

Slowly, I turn. Icy air melts through the hair on my head. On the ground the white ash drifts gently. My eyes stare, blinking, focusing.

'I've had enough of this,' I say aloud, and I do not recognise my own voice. 'Where are you?'

The ash is cloudy vapour, a thickening mist.

'Show yourself,' I demand.

'I will,' breathes a voice in my ear. 'I will. Though first be sure that you truly want to see me.'

A rustle behind me. I spin around quickly.

Amy sits alone, playing with her fingers. She murmurs a strange little song to herself. I decide what to do. I will lift her quickly and run. Away from here, from this part of the cemetery, as fast as I can. To the gates. I bend to pick her up.

'No!'

It is a screech.

'She's mine.'

I turn for the second time and sheer blind terror freezes me motionless. The tarpaulin rips back from the open grave and up out of it the lid of the chest crashes open. The fog pours in and down, and a roar and a fills the night.

A figure crawls out and rises above me. I feel my guts disintegrating, my mind breaking in terror.

Beside me Amy laughs. 'See, Solomon, the lady.'

I look wildly at the child. She is smiling and reaching out her hands. For the faintest second I see what she does. A gentle floating figure of a woman, stretching out her hands and humming a lilting tune.

And then the lips are drawn back from yellow teeth bared

in an evil snarl. Like a mad black dog. The watchman's dog.

My whole body is shuddering as I try to get control.

'What happened to the first workman,' I stutter. 'The one whose name was Joe?'

An arm reaches out and I stagger backwards. I see what I knew I would see. An arm with a deep cut sliced right across its wrist. Torn flesh and pus oozing from the wound. Drops of blood drip on the ground.

'The one whom first I called?' The voice hisses in the trees. 'I have him. As I will have you.

'Bowels. Brain. Blood and Bone.

'All.'

Joe's figure lurches towards me, a sickly smile on its curdled face.

'No!' I hold up my arms to fend it off.

Like an impressionist painting, it dissolves into a thousand different brush strokes. Then into small particles which now drift away into the ash, dissipating among the gravel paths.

I must move. I know this. I have to try to get away.

The juddering of my arms and legs means that I can barely walk, but I must. One foot in front of the other. Shaking all over and crying with fear.

'Amy,' my voice a ragged tear in the night. 'Amy, you have to come with me.'

'No,' she smiles at me.

'*No*,' says another voice inside my head.

'Yes.' I'm more determined now. 'Yes. What do you want with her, anyway?' I ask desperately. 'She's only a child.'

A child. A sick child. A little girl. Professor Miller's daughter.

'The miller's daughter,' I say aloud.

'Not my fault.' The whisper echoes round the graveyard. 'The miller himself to blame. He moved the river flow. Changing the course of running water is an evil thing to do. And a curse laid on cannot be easily lifted.'

'You cursed them all,' I shout. 'A malefice.'

There is a sharp cracking sound and the branch of a tree

comes down, narrowly missing my head.

'I know!' I scream out. 'I know it all! They burned you and you cursed them.'

The gravel on the path gathers before my eyes, collects and whirls at me, rattling on my face, scoring at my eyes.

I laugh like a crazy person. 'You were guilty. Most of them weren't. But not you. You were evil. *Are* evil.'

Something moves in my mind. A veil lifts. I step back. It advances towards me, within me.

'Know this.' It speaks inside my head. 'This has not come to pass by human design. *I* decided my time was now. The river will flow again as once it did. I've waited long for this. Years and centuries of reaching out, trying to grasp hold. Building my strength slowly. Touching other minds. Drawing first from visitors here, and then they came no more.'

I try to shut the voice out. Close off part of my mind. No use. It seeps in, like mist through a crack.

'Then into my orbit came youth. Drunken and drugged, but with untapped minds. It was so easy. I have gained a huge store.'

'I am not afraid,' I whisper to myself. 'I am not afraid.'

'Afraid? Afraid?' In the night air, a cackle as would freeze blood. Then there were eyes with the voice that I could hear all around me. Eyes which held mine. Hypnotic, drawing, drowning. The speech was slow and distinctive.

'No, not afraid. Not afraid. Terrified.'

The eyes changed. My world was spinning, hopeless and helpless. A voice spoke out, a woman's voice, clear and pure.

'EMOC DLIHC.'

And in my mind the runes unravelled. Whatever detached and singular part of me that could read the mirror writing.

'No, don't,' I ordered Amy. 'Do not go. Stay with me.'

Silence. Sudden and complete. Outside and in. I, with my mixed-up word order had understood the command.

I seize my chance in the small space I had been given.

Grasping Amy firmly by the wrist I drag her to her feet. She is heavy, reluctant to leave. Her body weight doubled, trebled by her unwillingness.

'Please,' I beg. Already I feel its return. Evil gathering its forces against me. 'Please, Amy, come with me.'

'Solomon!'

Someone calls my name. Right in my ear.

'Solomon!'

Long red fingernails grab my arm and dig into the flesh.

Chapter 25

'Solomon!'

The yell is from Ms Talmur who is standing beside me on the grass.

'How did you get here?' I gape at her, swaying on my feet.

'When you didn't come back to the police station I went to your house and spoke to your father. He didn't know where you were, but I guessed you would be here.' She looks around her wildly. 'There is something terrible going on. Isn't there?'

'It's here, all around us. Some awful evil thing.' The words are gabbling out of my mouth. 'I think it was burned and the ashes buried in a chest under the rowan tree.' I have to speak louder now to be heard. A wind has gathered. It is shaking the trees, howling through the branches.

'Dear God! What is that?' Ms Talmur grabs my arm again.

It is more than the noise of the wind that we hear. The howling is horrendous, a terrible baying noise, blocking out all other sounds, filling us up, tipping us towards madness.

'Let's try to get out.' Ms Talmur's teeth are chattering. She reaches out to Amy.

The child looks up. Her eyes are turned back in her head, her face deathly pale. Ms Talmur takes her hand. There is a hard laugh, and the child is wrenched from her. Ms Talmur is thrown aside. She screams and falls back awkwardly, cracking her head on an upright stone. Fear fills my heart. She lies broken on the ground, like a snapped-off flower stalk. I run to them, and then shout into the wind and noise.

'You have had enough. You have killed two people. You don't need any more. Let the child go.'

'I can't.'

There was a flicker there. I sensed a hesitation.

'Why not?'

'It is not for you to know.'

Somewhere in the labyrinth there is a closing off. So . . . What was there? A weakness?

I could only think to repeat what I had said.

'Let her go.'

'NO!' It is a howling cry. 'I need her.'

Need. Need? Why need? What is it that you must have?

There is an agitated jumble in my head. But I will not let go. 'I will not let you take her,' I shout out.

'You,' the voice states in deep derision, 'you. What are you?'

Don't listen. Don't listen. Don't listen. Don't.

'You are a stupid, lazy and ignorant boy.'

And it's Watkins that I hear. Him and every other teacher whose class I've been in.

'Thick-skulled, dim-witted, pudding head,' the belittling abuse goes on. 'Slow, backward, remedial, stupid, stupid, stupid.' The vile spittle streams out.

I stop then all right. That familiar creeping sensation of complete worthlessness. Humiliation. The sure and certain knowledge that no matter how hard I tried, no matter how well I did, it would never be good enough. I falter.

'Thick. Dull. Senseless. Dim-witted. Glaikit. Stupid.'

The sneering solidifies on me like congealing grease.

Stop, please stop. Make it stop. God. Anyone. Make it stop.

'How many times have I told you? Can't you remember anything? Stupid. Stupid. Stupid.'

I am standing in a pool of pee on the gym hall floor.

Stand in the corner. Stand in the waste bin. Stand off. Stand up – so that everyone can point at you. Stupid, stupid person.

I stumble on the grass. My head hangs low. I crumple to my knees. Amy whimpers. And that pathetic sound pulls me back.

'Solomon, don't cry.'

She floods me with strength.

'Whatever you are, YOU are nothing.' I think the thought deep inside my reason. 'You cannot be. And you will not be. You feed on hatred, greed, despair and frustration. But you do not exist as you once did. Why do you need the child?'

Innocent, pure, untouched.

'Not for you to know or understand.'

More revenge? It cannot be just that.

And suddenly I do know.

It was its other half. To be complete it needed a child's innocence, untouched, unsullied by the world. Her uncorrupt body and mind. To complete the circle. Then and only then could it walk the earth again. Walled in its tomb the soulless spirit languished. Joe had been consumed, with all his imperfections. Now the balance was needed to complete its release.

The knowledge gives me power.

'You will not have her.' I crawl towards Amy. If ever bravery was needed, it was needed now. 'You will NOT have her.'

'Then I will take her.'

I feel its presence now, deep inside me. Cold. Colder than any tomb.

'Beyond you. Past you. Through you. I will take her.'

And the thing before me, and in me, stretches out to suck me in.

I turn and grab Amy. I have no strength to lift or carry her. I wrap my arms about her and hold her fast.

There is a singing in the air. The wind drops and the leaves of the trees move in harmony. Beautiful music. The branches dip and sway in tune. I shut my mind off from it. I see the fog and the dark still night. Feel the cold through to my bones. Smell the dank reek of rotted flesh.

Amy strains against me, struggles with an extraordinary power. She unfastens the grip of my fingers one by one. Frees

109

herself from my grasp. I'm going to lose her. Whatever bewitchment is on her I cannot hold her to me.

Or can I?

'Amy.'

She is on the path now, a few paces distant. Walking towards the open grave.

'Amy.' I call again, softly. 'Remember the story I was telling you last night? You fell asleep before I finished. Don't you want to hear the end?'

She hesitates, glances back to me, then takes several steps forwards.

'The princess,' I say, keeping my voice low and even, 'the princess, with her long red-gold hair.' I let my mouth round out the vowels as I speak. My tongue rolls on the sounds of the words. 'The beautiful princess with her copper curls. Her hair was just like yours. Remember? And her loyal knights rode up to her castle gate. "You must come with us," they said, "and rescue your father." So early the very next morning, she saddled her favourite horse. The pure white mare with the silver star on its forehead, and as dawn was lighting the horizon, she rode out across the drawbridge . . ."'

I weave my web.

I spin my dream.

The child stops still again on the path.

'Would you like to know where the princess rode off to?' I ask her gently.

'Yes, Solomon,' she turns to me, 'yes.'

Chapter 26

There is an angry buzzing in my ears, but I go on.

'For many days and many nights the princess travelled westwards. Across the vast fields of waving corn, through tiny villages and hamlets . . .'

The air around me shimmers in fury and the earth starts to tremble. Amy is in front of me on the path, her face uptilted to mine and open with wonder. I realise that it is one of my father's stories that I am telling her, the sounds and the colours making music and rainbows inside her head.

' . . . she galloped along the dusty road towards the far mountains.'

The ground is shaking under my feet, but my voice is stronger and I take a pace or two backwards. Unbelievably, miraculously, Amy takes a few steps towards me, and I edge back again. Can I lead her out of the kirkyard like this?

'The mountains were high and dangerous, with steep slopes covered in the winter-time with a soft, deep, snow-fall.'

Two more paces. The grass withers as I walk. Something stalks beside me, but its footsteps leave no trace of its going. I retreat and Amy follows. I must put some distance between us and this focus of power. I know that we can resist it better the further away we are.

'As she and her loyal knights reached the gentle foothills the princess reined in her proud white mare . . .'

'Did her horse have a name, Solomon?' asks Amy.

'Yes,' I say.

What?

Quickly. Quickly. What?

'It was . . . it was called . . . Megan. Megan the Magnificent.' My heart is thudding in my ears.

'Solomon?'

Someone has murmured my name.

Shut it out, shut it out.

'Solomon.' Quietly this time. My eyes slide to the side. I cannot help it. To the direction of the sound.

'What's happening?'

It's Ms Talmur. Lifting her head, dazed and confused, gazing about her. My concentration falters.

No!

Behind Amy's head I see the white ash gather, coming together above where the chest lies, lid open.

NO!

The vile green liquid of a suppurating wound is pouring out, bubbling up from below.

'The horse . . .?' Amy asks again.

My gaze is transfixed beyond her. Hypnotised. Slowly she starts to turn her head.

'Solomon!' Ms Talmur speaks my name sharply. I snap round to look at her.

'What is it you see?' she demands.

I see her still sprawled on the ground, unable to get up. I see . . . before I turn back, compelled to look towards the grave . . . I see something glitter briefly in the grass. Amid the strewn contents of her handbag a make-up mirror gleams.

And it's in my hand.

There's a roaring in my ears, in my head.

'Look at me, Amy!' And I hold the mirror up, above her, to reflect back whatever is forming itself behind her.

The kirkyard itself is locked in the struggle. Earth and air tremble and shake. The mirror in my hand turns red-hot, and then the glass itself dissolves. It boils under my fingers and disintegrates. Scorches and burns my hand and I fling it from me.

'Don't leave me, Solomon.' Amy is weeping and she has

112

her arms clasped around my legs.

I crouch down beside her and pick her up. 'I won't. I won't,' I say. But there is little hope. I have no strength left. Neither in my legs or arms, nor in my heart or soul. Ms Talmur is half-sitting but cannot get to her feet. The tombstones are toppling. There is a deep rumbling from below us in the bowels of the earth. And I know that we are finished.

I sense the creeping decay move swiftly across the grass, smell the rotted stink of poison, taste the venom trickling into my mouth. It's coming now. For all of us.

And suddenly there's a different sound. A bellowing noise that vibrates from the walls and rings off the marble slabs. It's calling my name and rushing to help us. A great figure crashing up the long path from the main gate. Yelling its head off. Huge and clumsy and roaring like a lion.

My dad's voice, shouting at the stars.

'Hang on, Solomon. Hang on. I'm coming, Solomon.'

Chapter 27

He reaches me just as the storm breaks with a crash above our heads. The electricity in the air fuses with a tremendous crack, then descends to earth in a blinding sheet, bringing a tree down beside us. The clouds roll grumbling together. There is the briefest pause, then rain pours out of the sky in a sudden grey deluge.

'Hurry! Hurry!' My dad lifts Ms Talmur and swings her up and over his shoulder, fireman-carry style. I am still standing, stupefied at the sight of him. Wet through in seconds yet I hardly feel or see the downpour. My voice croaks out.

'How did you know to come here?' I ask, rain mingling with the tears on my face.

'The teacher came to the house to see if you were there,' he yells back over the sound of the wind. 'I came out to find you after she'd left. Searched everywhere. Then I saw her car parked on the road outside.'

'But . . . but how did you get in?' Slowly my brain is starting to unfreeze, unlock itself from whatever icy grip was on it.

'Padlocks are no bother to me,' he laughs, one of his great big happy laughs. 'I'll show you how to do that one day.'

Water is streaming down the tombstones, gathering in puddles, flowing along the paths.

'Take the little girl's other hand, Solomon,' my dad shouts as he grabs Amy by one arm. 'We don't have much time.'

What did he mean? He couldn't know what was happening here.

'Why?' I yell. 'What's wrong?'

'The river's in spate. It's running high because of all the rain. They're trying to sandbag it, but it's too late. Any minute now and it's going to overrun.'

I look back. Back to the wall, to the torn-down fencing and the wood behind. To where the river is, slightly to one side of us on the higher ground. And I knew now that the sound I had heard earlier was coming from there. The roaring of the water as it hurtled down from the rain-soaked hills. Every burn and stream choked and gushing with flood water. Carrying all before it. Small animals, trees, bushes, racing on to swell the flow. I can hear it now, above the gale and the sound of the wind tearing through the trees. Another noise, a surging pounding thunder which will not stay contained for much longer.

I take firm hold of Amy and start to follow my dad. She whimpers and stumbles and I haul roughly on her arm.

'Easy, son, easy.' My dad grins at me across her head.

I glance back quickly. 'If that goes . . .' I say.

'I know, I know.' He quickens his pace and takes longer strides.

I do as he does.

Always did.

Try to copy him. Be as big. Be as strong.

Never could.

I make my legs move faster, stretch them out.

And I do it.

Tonight I do it.

I am keeping up. We are running side by side.

The water is everywhere. Rivulets are running across the gray slabs, trickling among the carvings and the inscriptions, outlining their shape with a fleeting caress. My stones are weeping.

I can feel a strange shuddering beneath us, as if the river has found a passage underground and is even now gushing under our feet. Immediately in front of us a headstone falls, toppling onto the path, blocking our way.

MALEFICE.

My head rings like iron struck by a hammer. We will not be allowed to escape. The gravel on the path scatters and the earth moves beneath us.

'This place must be built on bog land. Watch your feet,' my dad shouts.

He steps across the fallen monument. I pick Amy up and clamber after him.

'Right, Sol,' he calls behind to me. 'One quick sprint for the gate.'

It's lying open as he left it on his way in. I keep my eyes on his back, Ms Talmur helpless, slumped across his shoulders. He is through, across the road and heading for the higher ground on the other side.

I am following. I see him getting smaller. Through the wrong end of a telescope. Smaller and smaller.

My bones in my legs are heavy, the blood thickening and congealing in my veins. I am walking through mud. It's round my ankles and pulling me down. Thick and green and pus-yellow. Dragging me under, reaching up, choking, smothering. The cloth from the stone urn is billowing above me, settling on my shoulders, draping itself across my face. Flowing down and around. Choking, smothering.

The gate to freedom is in front of me, just out of reach, beyond my grasp. Slowly closing.

'Dad! Help me!' I shriek.

There is an insistent murmuring in my ears.

Lie down. Rest. Just for a moment.

A whispering in my ear.

Sleep. Close your eyes. Sleep.

A soft breath on my cheek.

Rest now, just for a second.

A rustling hush inside my head.

I sink slowly into the mud, slide gently down. Behind me, with a thunderous crash, the river burst its banks.

Chapter 28

On my knees, with my arms round Amy, I see death surging towards us. A wall of water is pouring through the dyke at the far end. White-flecked, dark and dreadful, nothing will stand in its way. It slows, but only for a moment, at the deep gouge in the ground under the wall. Crashing down into the bowels of the earth, swilling out the pit, boiling and foaming like fury.

A hellish screech rends the air. A desolate wailing that reverberates off the tombstones, inside my skull and out and up to the sky.

Like the cleansing of an underground sewer by flooding, the river has dispersed the contents of that grave into a million different atoms. The high-pitched banshee yell continues, long drawn-out, thinner, higher. The air shivers and splinters like shattered crystal.

Then it's gone.

Into the silence.

Trailing as an echo.

Whispers spin off into the void. Plucked from all about us. Inside and out. Dispersed and dying, they fade to nothing.

And suddenly the kirkyard is silent. And black night is racing at me.

My head snaps back. Cold reality returns like the lifting of an enchantment.

My father is shouting my name as he runs towards me. Ms Talmur is screaming. I gather Amy up and turn and run.

The water hits me in the back with the force of a huge fist. I fall forward but keep a desperate grip of Amy. It's over my head, blocking my nose and ears. I'm drowning.

Huge mouthfuls of filthy liquid are being forced down my throat. I'm spluttering and gasping. I can't see. Amy is almost wrenched from my grasp but I hang on to her. There's a pounding noise in my ears, my fingers slacken . . .

Then there are strong arms round my shoulders, pulling us up. Big hands grab my skinny wrists and start to haul me up the hill. I'm scrambling on my hands and knees.

The water surges again and a great wave breaks over my head and the downpull drags us back. But Ms Talmur has Amy in her arms now and my dad has hoisted me out of the torrent, his arm around my waist. Now we're struggling waist-high, and then we're wading knee-deep in water. And then further up the slope it's slopping round our ankles and we're clear.

We hang on to each other, laughing and crying. Amy stretches out her hands to me and I take her, and she wraps her arms round my neck.

'Is she gone?'

The question only I can hear.

'For ever,' I say firmly.

We look down at the widening lake of water below us, with just the tops of the trees showing, and floating debris everywhere. Far back where the dyke and the rowan tree once stood do I see, or imagine, a silent whirlpool? A black spinning column of water being sucked down and down.

If the rowan tree had not been cut down, would none of this have happened? I wonder. It is an ancient superstition, the rowan as a protection against evil.

"Rowan tree and red thread
Make the malefice dead."

Ms Talmur reads this out from a book to me one day, weeks later. 'It's a Norse legend,' she says. 'The rowan is supposed to have sprung from the feather of the bird which stole fire from the gods and brought it to earth. So the red berries were a charm against evil.' She looks at me, and speaks quietly. 'We

118

were right, Solomon, weren't we? There was something amiss in that graveyard.'

I nod.

'And it wasn't just our imagination,' she says slowly. 'I began to think it was, you see. When both you and Amy had red markings on your skin, and were feverish, I thought it was because you had heard about the smallpox, and were worried about catching it.'

No, I think. Not our own imagination playing tricks on us. Something else using our imagination against us both.

'But it's gone now, hasn't it? Swept away by the flowing river?'

'I suppose so,' I say.

'And now that the place has been cleared, and everything relocated, it's finished.'

I nod. I've decided I'm telling no one about the chest. They might decide to try and find it. And it's better where it is, undisturbed. They said the first workman ran off with another woman or something, and the second was drunk and fell in the river and drowned. But I know. So does Amy. They told her she had been delirious because she was ill, and had wandered off. Said she had a bad dream. We were in the hospital together overnight. She looked over at me when the doctor told her this. I smiled at her and she smiled back.

When I got home the next day the whisky bottle was still sitting on the kitchen table. It was full.

So he hadn't drunk any that night when I'd asked him not to. Just as well. I wouldn't be here now if he had. He must know that.

He saw me staring at it as we both came into the kitchen.

'I'll try,' he said. 'I'll do my best, but I'm not making any promises I can't keep.'

I took it outside our back door. There is a drain there beside the step. I dropped it down. The bottle crashed and the amber liquid ran away. I went back inside.

He gave a big sigh. 'Fancy a cup of tea?'

Chapter 29

'Let's put the cards and books away and go for a walk.'

Ms Talmur gathered up all my papers and drawings and shoved them away in a folder. There'd been something on her mind since our lesson started. My attention, not good at any time, made worse by her shifting restlessly about in her chair. The constant movement of her hands, fingers twisting through the ends of her hair.

And always slow. Deadly slow. I look at the words on the page, at my crabbed writing carefully spaced out on alternate lines, and I know I should remember what they mean. I reach around inside my head and it's not there.

Then she tells me. Smiling patiently. And I recall that she told me that word yesterday, and the day before, and the day before that . . . .

Embarrassment and humiliation are on my face, a sour taste in my mouth.

'It's no good,' I say.

'Yes, it is,' she says firmly.

The words tremble on the page. I shake my head. The ragged black hole of despair widening in and around me. Rage rushing in fast to fill up the void.

'No,' I shout.

'Did Sir Edmund Hillary give up on the slopes of Everest?' she demands. 'Did Captain Scott turn back? Did Columbus? Did Ezekial McGribbons?'

I fall for it.

'Who's Ezekial McGribbons?'

'I don't know. I made him up, didn't I?'

I laugh and we start again.

And again.

And again.

'Will it ever come right?' I ask.

She meets my eyes and doesn't look away. 'Not completely,' she says. 'When you're rich and famous, don't ever write out a cheque without having someone make sure that your numbers are correct.' She laughs. 'You'd be just as likely to put down 3,000 pounds as 300.' She puts her hand on my arm. 'But you CAN cope with it. Enough to get by. Remember it's a difficulty, not a disability. You must move past it and get on with your life. Do what you want to do.' Her nails are through the wool of my jumper. 'You control it, not the other way around.'

Rich and famous, I think. Lots of rich and famous people have my problem. She's told me often enough. But I'm not rich or famous. I'm ordinary and it doesn't help me a lot to know about them.

She's watching me. 'You shouldn't try to hide behind a medical diagnosis, or use it as an excuse.

'There's a theory that people with learning difficulties are compensated in other ways, their energy channelled somewhere else. Into the Arts for example. Like Cher and Tom Cruise.'

'You think I could become an actor?'

'You'll have to find out for yourself. Search out your own particular talent.'

'Supposing I don't have any?'

'Speaking realistically, you might not be specially gifted in one area, but your drawings have an unusual originality, now that you've stopped copying how other people hold their pencil. It might develop, I don't know . . .' She brushes her hair back from her face. 'Please don't think of it as winning or losing. You have to realise it's not your *fault*. And it's you that's important. And for better or worse this is part of you, like the colour of your eyes or the shape of your nose.'

'Realistically.' I think of the word. 'Rea . . . Rea . . .

Rea . . .' moving as the sea, like the tide coming in. 'Rea . . .' The waves rushing to shore. 'Listic . . . listic' they smash on the rocks, 'ally . . .' the spray flying high into the air. 'Realistically!'

No other adult I know would have used such a long and complicated word when talking to me. They all use small words, short sentences and speak slowly. They think I won't understand the big words because I'm clumsy, and make mistakes when reading and writing.

We go for our walk.

Now we're outside and on the path behind the school leading into the woods. There's an early moon in the sky, a pale piece of watered silk. We go by the river to where the new bridge with its triple arches spans the water. We sit on the grass at the shingly edge and watch a family of ducks calling noisily to each other. Red fire from the setting sun making the surface molten glass.

A beautiful evening.

'I'm leaving,' she says.

My brain stops. Just like that. One second I was thinking about ducks and water. Then the next second, nothing.

'The headteacher gave me a terrific reference. Remember our experiment in the gym hall that day with the parents of the new intake? Well, the man in the brown suit wrote and told the head that he was incorporating my ideas into one of his staff training modules. I've been offered a promotion,' she hesitates. 'In another school.'

'Yeah?'

What'm I gonna do. Do. Without you. You.

Who cares? I don't.

'Please don't look at me like that, Solomon.'

She's the only one who ever called me that.

Solomon.

I shrug. 'No problem,' I say.

She looks as though she might either cuff my head or put her arm round my shoulders. I start to get up.

'Wait,' she pulls my sleeve. 'It's better for you. Believe me. You're already beginning to rely on me too much, and I won't be here for the rest of your life. You've got to do it on your own, and the sooner the better.'

Now I look at her desperately. I can hear the tears in my voice. 'I need help.'

'I'll get you help,' she says gently. 'I'll arrange for another tutor.'

'I don't want another tutor.'

'I know, and that's one of the reasons I'm going.' She points at the river bank. 'See the ducklings there. Eventually they swim by themselves. If I don't go soon, then you might not learn to swim by yourself. I couldn't do that to you. You're too important to me.'

Words like pebbles plopping in the water. Stones falling, down, down in the darkness, to lie on the river bed.

Same as Peter had said, I thought suddenly. My rock. Telling me it was better to do it on my own.

'You've faced up to your dyslexia, Solomon,' Ms Talmur went on. 'Now you've got to keep moving forward. The unique individual that you finally become you will have made yourself.'

She leans forward and traces in the shingle with her forefinger.

'See,' she says, 'how the river flows. It curves as it leaves the town. "S" like a snake.' She tilts her head back so that her face is turned towards the sky.

'Then, a circle for the sun. The sun by day.'

"o"

'Now, the tree by the water's edge. A silver birch, tall and straight.'

"l"

'The moon by night.'

"o"

'Start to cross the bridge, until you reach the second arch.'

"m"

'Again the sun and moon.'

"o"

'The last arch of the bridge. Now you are safely at the end.'

"n"

She has written my name in the earth.

Solomon.

'It will be difficult for you, very difficult. There will always be people who won't understand. And others seeking a focus for their own frustration. They'll come after you, Solomon. You are an easy target. You're going to have to be strong.'

I stare at the ground. 'Sometimes, it's too hard. The struggle, too difficult.'

'You *are* strong. You resisted whatever evil force tried to seduce you and Amy. You fought back. And all those years before, in school. The torture and frustration. You didn't do drugs or hide yourself in drink. You can do it. And it will make you better. Like the furnace flame. The hotter the forge, the sharper the edge.'

She puts her arm around my shoulder.

'Please, Solomon. Don't ever be the same as anyone else.'

Chapter 30

I have to cross the bridge to get to the town hall. The sound of running water is reassuring. I stop in the middle of the bridge and look around me. In my hand is the gold wedding ring. I thrust my fist through the railings, unclench my fingers and let go.

The river, dark brown and silent, flows swift and thick under the arches. There is a part on the far side, just by one of the supports, where the water stagnates. Dead fish float there, belly up, and nothing grows on the muddy verge. I don't go there. The water is greasy and the air hangs over it, dank and cold.

Down deep is where the chest lies.

Gathering strength.

Waiting.

For another time.

I run on.

The evening is creeping softly across the sky, the air cool on my face. I wait at the intersection for a gap in the traffic and then dodge across the road. It starts to rain, a light falling of water that lies as fine mist on my hair and cheeks. The cars hiss quietly as they pass. The colours of the traffic lights are reflected from the pavement back to me. A coat of many hues spread out on the ground for me to tread on.

I might go and visit my mother. Talk. Find out about her properly. The sort of stuff she likes to do. What makes her laugh. Ask her things.

I always thought that if I saw her again I would ask her why she left. Now I don't need to ask her that. Now I know.

It was too much. She couldn't handle it any more. Maybe I

won't be able to either.

If he doesn't go to the meeting tonight . . .

It's the first step. Admit what you are. Accept that your problems are part of yourself. Know them. Know yourself. Then deal with them.

Ultimately it is yourself you face. If you can.

Truth comes in all sorts of ways. A great surge of self-knowing, like a chasm opening up under your feet, or a slow dawning of realisation. Shapes fitting piece by piece. Life . . . doing a jigsaw with the picture missing. Fumbling for the correct piece. Will you ever really know for sure that you got it right?

The mirror I held up in the graveyard boiled and disintegrated because there was nothing truly there to see. To behold itself incomplete and without hope, would mean self-destruction. How many others, every drab day, avoid their own reflection?

Now . . .

I wait for him outside the meeting hall. In the grey smirring drizzle. My hands are cold. I pull the sleeves of my jumper down over my fingers. Can he do it? Will he come?

I don't know. I step inside. Into the orange glow and the smell of stewed tea.

Deep within the building the notes of a ratchety piano sound. A voice calls out dance steps. A cleaner's bucket clatters and I hear laughter. The small tattered notice on the green baize board says the alcoholics meeting is downstairs.

I lean against the door and peer outside through the window, up the street. My breath condenses on the etched glass panel. I start to write. Slowly, awkwardly, I trace my fingers on the steamed-up surface.

First, the curved letter, slithering from top to bottom.

S.

Next . . . a circle.

The sun by day, and the moon by night.

Now I have to cross my bridge.

I make the letters.
Carefully and complete.
Solomon, my name.

A Selected List of Fiction from Mammoth

While every effort is made to keep prices low, it is sometimes necessary to increase prices at short notice. Mandarin Paperbacks reserves the right to show new retail prices on covers which may differ from those previously advertised in the text or elsewhere.

The prices shown below were correct at the time of going to press.

☐	7497 0343 1	**The Stone Menagerie**	Anne Fine	£2.99
☐	7497 1793 9	**Ten Hours to Live**	Pete Johnson	£3.50
☐	7497 0281 8	**The Homeward Bounders**	Diana Wynne Jones	£3.50
☐	7497 1061 6	**A Little Love Song**	Michelle Magorian	£3.99
☐	7497 1482 4	**Writing in Martian**	Andrew Matthews	£2.99
☐	7497 0323 7	**Silver**	Norma Fox Mazer	£3.50
☐	7497 0325 3	**The Girl of his Dreams**	Harry Mazer	£2.99
☐	7497 1699 1	**You Just Don't Listen!**	Sam McBratney	£2.99
☐	7497 1849 8	**Prices**	David McRobbie	£3.50
☐	7497 0558 2	**Frankie's Story**	Catherine Sefton	£2.99
☐	7497 1291 0	**The Spirit House**	William Sleator	£2.99
☐	7497 1777 7	**The Island and the Ring**	Laura C Stevenson	£3.99
☐	7497 1685 1	**The Boy in the Bubble**	Ian Strachan	£3.50
☐	7497 0009 2	**Secret Diary of Adrian Mole**	Sue Townsend	£3.50
☐	7497 1015 2	**Come Lucky April**	Jean Ure	£3.50
☐	7497 1824 2	**Do Over**	Rachel Vail	£3.50
☐	7497 0147 1	**A Walk on the Wild Side**	Robert Westall	£3.50

All these books are available at your bookshop or newsagent, or can be ordered direct from the address below. Just tick the titles you want and fill in the form below.

Cash Sales Department, PO Box 5, Rushden, Northants NN10 6YX.
Fax: 01933 414047 : Phone: 01933 414000.

Please send cheque, payable to 'Reed Book Services Ltd.', or postal order for purchase price quoted and allow the following for postage and packing:

£1.00 for the first book, 50p for the second; **FREE POSTAGE AND PACKING FOR THREE BOOKS OR MORE PER ORDER.**

NAME (Block letters) ....

ADDRESS ....

....

☐ I enclose my remittance for ....

☐ I wish to pay by Access/Visa Card Number ☐☐☐☐☐☐☐☐☐☐☐☐☐☐☐☐

Expiry Date ☐☐☐☐

Signature ....

Please quote our reference: MAND